THE BUNNY
THAT TOOK OVER
THE WORLD

STEVEN
OLSEN

BUNNY
MUFFIN
BOOKS

ISBN 978-0-9906119-0-5 (hardcover)
ISBN 978-0-9906119-1-2 (paperback)
ISBN 978-0-9906119-2-9 (ebook)

Fonts used:
Adobe Garamond Pro 12 point
Metro 24 point
Heavy Data 24 and 18 point
AR Christy 24 point

Entypo pictograms by Daniel Bruce (entypo.com)
Batch pictograms by Adam Whitcroft
Heydings Icons by Heydon Pickering
Keyamoon Icons by Keyamoon

Also available as an Ebook

For my family and friends who supported me and my bunnies all the way, all the time. Thank you all so much.

CHAPTER

1

"To put it simply, he's too good to be true."

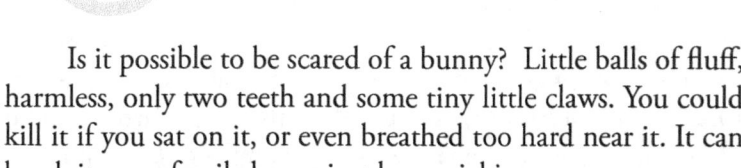
–Cory Yalk, Technology News.

Is it possible to be scared of a bunny? Little balls of fluff, harmless, only two teeth and some tiny little claws. You could kill it if you sat on it, or even breathed too hard near it. It can break its own fragile bones just by panicking.

Bunnies panic a lot.

Yet, people were scared of Lysander. That was his name, Lysander. The humans didn't know that, of course, and so gave him their own name. They called him Glossy. And he was. Fur of platinum silk, sleeked down in tufts across his shiny coat. Bright wet nose and brighter eyes. The face framed by velvet ears giving it the look of innocent wonder.

The perfect bunny.

It was odd; most of the other bunnies born in the litter with him weren't perfect. No, they were merely average. Their fur didn't seem to repel dirt and their claws had to be clipped. Not a single one had even a feather of white fur. Of course, they still sold. Sold to families that would keep them in little hutches behind their houses, securely in place for life. They were destined to go through bags and bags of pellets, sold from the store that had sold them. They never truly left that store, always within an hour's drive, always getting their food and supplies from the same place.

But Glossy never even left the store. He stayed, after the very last baby bunny was sold. Then his parents were sold, too. He didn't even seem depressed, he just . . . stared. Stared across at the aisle directly in front of his glass cage. The treat section. The store workers once gave him some of the treats, but he didn't touch them. He didn't ever eat anything besides his little pellets of crushed hay and plants. He was simply staring, not a single thought in his soft, white head. No care for treats. Clueless. He never moved, except on his routine visits to three spots in his cage. One was his water spigot, he would drink on the hour. One was his food bowl, where he ate five times a day. One was his restroom, also used hourly. The fourth, unused corner had a salt lick. He never nibbled on the cage, or did anything to dull his claws. They always stayed the perfect length. Employees wondered whether they grew.

He was flawless. Never a mistake, never an interruption to the routine.

But nobody bought him. Not for three whole years. He stayed in that little cage, day in, day out. Drew Howell, the store owner, tried everything. He put Glossy on sale, offered a free cage and a three month supply of food. But nobody bought him. Soon it became a matter of pride. Drew had never had a problem like this before, and he swore he would sell Glossy no matter what.

They said he was too clean, that he wouldn't live in a hutch. They said they couldn't care for a show rabbit or that maybe a hamster would be better after all. Any possible excuse was used, and the children always backed up the parents.

The employees always expected screams and demands when a certain pet couldn't be bought, but after seeing Glossy, a child would rather have anything else. And looking at that bunny, the employees knew why.

It simply didn't have a soul. It was a robot, going through the motions. Except unlike a machine, it didn't build anything. It didn't have any point. Petting it gave no reaction, it never seemed to take any happiness at all from anything they tried, and it just seemed to not care. It was an honest to goodness machine, and it terrified people. People came to the pet shop to buy something they could love, not a pellet-eating robot.

Drew often spent his free time in that very aisle, staring right back at Glossy, wondering. He waved his hand in front of Glossy's face, tapped the glass, even shouted once. He even had an employee film him as he popped off a firework not an inch away from Glossy's ears. They watched the film, knowing what they would see. They saw nothing, of course. Glossy didn't twitch, didn't blink. Absolutely nothing.

Drew should have just ordered new bunnies, released Glossy to the wild and been done with him. He wasn't going to be purchased, Drew knew. He wasn't even going to be petted, ever. He was going to live, and then die, in that little roundabout path of his life. Drew wouldn't have been surprised if Glossy did die, and his body just sat there, staring. After that, Drew had to check Glossy's pulse every time he walked past, just to make sure. It was still there, the little heart still popping off a fast heartbeat, just like a perfect bunny's heart should be. Glossy was still going.

Glossy wasn't ever going to change.

CHAPTER 2

"I was born by lightning, forged by impossible luck and unbearable pain."

–Lysander

The town that held the pet shop, Helaman Valley, looked like a mud slide. It snuggled right in between two mountains, in the deep canyon splitting the range in two. The houses slid out of the canyon, exiting the steep slope like thick syrup, and floated down until they hit the highway.

That highway was the dividing line, a solid stripe of white with the brown-black town on one side, neon signs buzzing. The other side held a cut-and-paste assortment of farm blocks. It was hay farms, all of it, and in the summer it rotated in an endless cycle of yellow and green, an agricultural chessboard. Cow sheds dotted the farms as the pieces. Milk trucks trundled off the highway to pick up milk and ship it off to the rest of the wide world outside the valley. The highway seemed to be protecting the farms from the sludge of civilization draining out of the canyon. Cars buzzed across it every day, but few got off or on.

This was only Helaman Valley, a town with a whole lot of gas stations and people to run them. A place to get fuel, and get away. No one really cared.

And that's why they didn't see it coming. If they cared, a weatherman would have noticed the gathering clouds, the pressure front. They would have seen the wind before it blew down that canyon and hit the town, ripping it to shreds in the middle of the night.

There wasn't any warning, no drifting newspapers except mere seconds before. And then it was there. The pitch-colored cloud layer above turned into a frenzy of rain. The cars on the highway began to drift to the side, struggling to stay between the lines. Dogs yipped and scrambled for cover as the trash lying on the ground took flight.

It grew from there.

Leaves began to stream out from trees as they bent into bows, groaning under the pressure. Smaller objects began to overturn, yard toys tumbling down the streets. Cars were pulled to the sides of the roads, people barging into the nearest house without even bothering to knock.

Trees began to crack, splinters of life pulled off by the wind as the corpse crashed to the earth it fed from. The trees around the pet shop quaked, a sound so low that it was felt more than heard. One, a massive oak, the biggest in all of town, made a shocking crack, the sound of wood shattering. It held for the moment, but leaned in towards the wall.

Power lines began to break, electricity snapping and fizzing before disappearing. Lights in houses snapped off minutes after the people woke up and switched them on. The wind was so strong several roofs came clear off, sending screaming families to huddle in the basement.

Meanwhile, in the dark pet store, animals began to shift. They could hear the muffled wind, feel it beating on the building, and instinct told them of danger.

Glossy woke up.

It wasn't much, in comparison to a normal bunny. But this was the first time in almost three years that Glossy had broken his routine. He slept all night, no exceptions. But something, deep inside, was stirring. Glossy's heart picked up, a mere fraction faster.

Then, there was the muffled sound of wood snapping. Something shuddered, sending a small tremor through the store. And then it came through the wall. The big oak was coming down. It hit the front wall, taking it along with a clod of roof. Fish tanks against the wall burst. Guppies flapped frantically as they sailed through the air just ahead of the oncoming branches. The oak hit the first shelf, crashing to a halt.

The animals were going berserk. The fish flopped up and down on the ground, doomed. The tree had stopped. It was, thankfully, nowhere near any animals besides the fish. The wind poured through the crack, flinging pet supplies everywhere, dry food pouring across the ground.

Then, metal began to squeal. The shelf began to creak, tipping. The metal supports holding it to the ceiling snapped, giving underneath the corpse of the tree. The shelf collapsed in half, jumping forward and hitting the next. That shelf screamed as it became part of the chain reaction.

Glossy's shelf was next.

Glossy felt gravity give and an invisible hand throw his cage forward. His eyes widened and his heart jumped, tripping over itself as it tried to beat faster than it had during Glossy's entire life. His breath quickened and his nose shivered. For the first time in his three years of life, Glossy felt fear.

Gravity came back. Glossy hit the ground just after the exploding wall of his cage. Glass flew through the air, deadly

knives that shot in every direction. Glossy could only close his eyes, curling up his fragile body in the only way he knew for protection. His body rolled, and he could hear screaming metal above and pet supplies pouring down. Toys and treats cascaded over it all. Glossy convulsed, curling up. Ancient instinct flooded his body, killing all hopes of routine, any happy nirvana he had had before.

When the chaos stopped for a moment, replaced by the white noise of the wind, Glossy uncurled and looked around. He was under a shelf, propped up against another. A thin metal band held fifty pounds of dog food, just above Glossy's head. His cage was in shards around him. For a second, Glossy sat up, staring. But then he twitched, realizing he was in the middle of a catastrophe, and crouched low. Instinct gripped his mind with shuddering, heart-twitching fear.

Animals howled, hissed, screamed. Fish splashed. Glossy turned, looking, looking for the bright yellow uniform of the store workers. But at night, they were all home. There was no one there to help, no one there to fix his cage.

Glossy ran for open space, panting and already feeling exhausted. His lungs felt like he was breathing ice water, refusing to cooperate with his uncoordinated legs. His feet burned, leaving tiny blood spots on the tile.

Some other animals had also lost their cages. All the reptiles and most of the cats were free, glass cages shattered, wire broken and doors sprung wide. The ones able to move were running, hopping, or scurrying toward the exit. They fought against the wind, longing for air and sun, which before they had only seen through windows. Looking for sunlight in the rain. Glossy followed, fueled by panic and fear. He was lost amidst the panic. His nose picked up something other than wood shavings. Sweat, cold sweat. Animal fear.

The instant he was out of the gap in the wall, the wind hit him. Most animals were shoved a little, but his thin body proved no match for the crosswinds. He went tumbling end over end, flying across the road and slamming into a house porch. Glossy slumped to the ground, hurting all over. His only thought was one of pure, unmistakable fear, tempered by pain. He looked up to the dark, cloudy sky. Lightning flashed from black clouds, blasting open the ground. Flocks of bats, their feeding interrupted, flapped uselessly back and forth in the wind. Even they hadn't realized the weather in time, and were paying for it. Not a human was in sight, except for the cars on the highway, sliding and slowing down so they wouldn't join the jumble of already crashed cars.

Then, lightning struck a telephone pole. Its top exploded in a storm of wiring and static. The cords began to sweep downward, and as they did, they connected, flashing out columns of electricity. As Glossy stared, he saw something impossible.

One bat had been separated, the wind playing with him not unlike how dogs played with chew toys. The bat, out of control, had run right into the power lines. It was blasted backwards in an arc of fiery light, landing smoking in the middle of the street. Glossy could only stare, no idea of what to do, no idea of whether to give into instinct, and run, or cower, or something else.

Then, he saw it coming. The truck, down the road, and heading straight for the bat. Glossy stared in horror, seeing it coming. The bat just laying there. Glossy stared into the blinding headlights, his mind freezing as his eyes tried to dilate, failing to adjust properly. Everything seemed to be swimming on the air. He knew he had to run, instinct screamed at him that he had to run. Glossy turned, muscles bunching, ready to head into darkness. Then he aborted, spinning around and facing the car again.

He remembered something.

And then Glossy did something a bunny would never do. He ran forward, into the road. He went straight for the downed bat. He reached him seconds before the truck. He looked at the tires, bit the bats foot.

Pulled.

The tire ripped past, spraying a deluge of water into Glossy's face. The tires had passed on either side. Glossy stared around, and then began to drag the bat's limp body across the road, pulling it towards the darkness under the porch he had slammed against. There they would be safe. They could wait out the storm. He would live.

What Glossy didn't notice was that he was pulling the bat past the power lines. The wind picked up the wires, snapping them and sending sparks through the air. They flew right past Glossy.

And then, one connected. Glossy straightened, felt the electric circuit connect through his body, and the world turned off.

CHAPTER 3

"Well, even I was kind at first. You can't tell a freak just by looks."

–Darshep

Glossy, or Lysander, groaned. The voice didn't stop. It muttered behind the thoughts of his head, swimming up through pain and wooziness. Slowly, he opened his eyes. The world shook for a moment, like the water in his water dish when he drank. The entire world had felt like a water dish for three days now. Finally it focused.

"You'll be okay?" The soft voice asked, and a huge white bunny stepped into Lysander's vision, crouching down to see into his eyes, "Hungry?"

Lysander considered the question for a long time, his thoughts beating in tune with his pounding head. He saw behind the bunny a long sky and a lowering hill, tumbling down to the canyon and the very close city. He could see the highway from here. Just about a foot below, water rushed. What had the others called it? Waterlog, that was it. Someplace they called Haven was just above. Haven, the rabbit burrows, right above Waterlog. Lysander looked around, seeing the tumble of waterfalls, one after another. It was beautiful, so beautiful it almost made his pain go away for a second. He sat about three feet

above the river, on an outcropping of soft, wet grass. The smell even pleased him. A smell he didn't recognize. The pet shop didn't smell anything like this.

Of course, he wasn't near the pet shop anymore. He could see it from where he was, down below. It was lost somewhere in the spiky roofs of Helaman Valley. But this was nothing like it. Lysander wasn't completely sure how he had gotten here. They had found him, they said. Some bunnies had gotten lost in the storm, and had found him, alone, in town. They had gotten help, and hid him under a porch for a while. Then, when Lysander had been half-awake, they had led him up the mountain to Waterlog. He could only remember that as an endless march uphill. They had promised food, and his hunger had made him go all the way up, past trees and everything.

"No, I'm alright." He said softly, actually surprised his voice worked so well. He hadn't used it since his parents were sold. He almost thought he had forgotten how to.

"Right… Alright." The rabbit took a few steps backward, cocking her head, "I'm Mirada, by the way… you feeling better yet?" Her eyes drifted to the side, around where Lysander's ear was. All the bunnies did that. That's what Lysander had noticed, the very first thing. He had awoken here, head hurting and pain flashing through his skull. It came quickly and blasted across, like lightning. That's all he could remember, something about lightning. He remembered a storm, and his escape. Then chaos, and a bat… had he really rescued that bat? It was so fuzzy. Then lightning. He had been struck by lightning, he knew he had. That's what it had felt like. Or at least, what he imagined lightning to be.

Then, in the morning, or several mornings later, he had awoken to Mirada, poking him with her nose and smiling a lot. He did remember her in his rescue party, though he could barely remember a thing. Every time he tried the lightning would buzz him again, nearly causing him to faint. It didn't matter, though. He was safe here, or so they told him. Not any lightning or storms, very few predators, whatever those were.

"Better?" Mirada prompted again, her eyes wide. She wouldn't stop annoying him. She seemed to be everywhere, like a slave to Lysander.

He sighed, the motion hurting his lungs, "Not yet."

Mirada stared at him a little longer, before hopping a few steps away. She turned back to say, "I'll get some grass roots." She smiled widely, hesitated for a second, and left.

Lysander breathed out and in slowly, concentrating on not stressing himself. His entire body pounded with pain and aches, washing out from his brain. When the sun came out, when it truly became morning and the sun broke some tiny rays through the cloud layer, he'd feel better. That's all he had managed to do for the past three days since the storm. He'd come out, and lay in the sun, trying to sleep so the headaches might leave for a moment.

What was wrong with him, anyway? It was visible, every bunny that saw him, every bunny that watched him limp slowly everywhere, stared at a spot on his head. Something had happened, but Lysander couldn't tell. He wished for one of those things in the pet shop, those walls that reflected you. He'd use the river, if it wasn't rushing over stones and cascading down in so much chaos.

It didn't matter, now, though. Lysander sighed, not knowing what to think. What was he doing here? Why had he survived, anyway? All he could manage to do was sit outside for maybe half a day, eat some plants, and sleep for most of the day

and night.

Why had this happened? Lysander asked himself. He was content in the pet store. Wasn't he?

He couldn't remember. There were vague memories of other bunnies, which slowly disappeared one by one. He knew two of them as his parents. He had loved his parents. They had all treated him so kindly, like the bunnies here did. Did that mean he was sick back then, too? He felt sick thinking about it. So sick he could puke. He had mentioned this to Mirada, but she told him rabbits didn't puke. Cats seemed to do it all the time, though.

Then what? After all the bunnies were gone, Lysander's memory was gone completely. He had some vague feeling of a long time passing, but exact memories were impossible. He also got the feeling that he might not want to remember, and so tried to forget about it even more.

Even without memories, Lysander wanted the store back. He wanted his cage, his bedding. He leaned sideways into the ground, trying to rub his head in it and pretend it was soft wood chips. But it was wet, squishing grass. The cold made his head pound more, and he retracted quickly, which caused black spots to dance across his eyes, and he tried not to panic. That wouldn't help. It never did. Instead, he managed to calm himself and look out at the city. The cars buzzed back and forth across the highway. Lysander hated cars. What kind of beast just tried to crush things for no reason? Maybe the car had been trying to eat him. Lysander could understand that. Dogs in the store would have eaten him, given the chance. Mirada had told him things out here would like to eat him too.

But those cars… Lysander somehow doubted they had any intention of eating him. Something told him they were confined to those lines of rock they ran across, zipping by those big walls and buildings. All of them were covered in those strange symbols and pictures. As Lysander looked, he began to remember symbols, painted across the products in the store. He closed his eyes, willing them to go away, but they didn't. They kept on going, spinning around, reshaping and popping in front of his vision. Trying to get his attention and causing his headache to flare in response.

It was almost as if they were trying to tell him something.

CHAPTER 4

"He destroyed everything I had, then turned around and gave me something better. I guess I have to thank him."

–Drew Howell

"I could have sworn… and he's missing, too." Drew said, getting on his hands and knees again to look under the collapsed shelf, "Don't see him, anyhow."

"Maybe he ran away, Mr. Howell." Zach said, still holding that mop in his characteristic way, leaning on it like a skater leaning up against a wall, eyes half-closed. It was a good thing he was just a teenager, and not in charge of the pet store. Sure, maybe Drew was a worrier, but that meant he cared. Cared about the animals. Zach didn't.

Drew kicked some dry food across the floor. He took a few steps, moving broken toys and rubbish out of the way with his feet. Shuffling, a man near death. The whole shop smelled like a sick cross between cat food and fish water. That was a normal smell for the shop, actually, but when it was this strong Drew wanted to retch. He said, "Glossy wouldn't have run. He would have sat right there. Probably wouldn't even wake up until it was time to open the store. I know he would have stayed."

"He probably got scared." Zach said, "But what about the

puppies? They're worth like, three hundred dollars, right? We should be looking for them. And you couldn't even sell that bunny!"

"That's why..." Drew stood up, shaking his head and gently inspecting his hands for glass. Why was he frustrated? He looked sadly over the shelves. A mini lake full of bloated animal food sopped the ground, dead fish bobbing on the top, "What a mess."

"I hope you're paying me overtime!" Zach joked, and began to laugh before he saw the look on Drew's face, "Sorry, Mr. Howell... that wasn't the best thing to say."

"No, I'll pay you." Drew said, shrugging, "Like always. But you might not have to clean up, anyway."

"Why not, sir? I mean, gotta be clean. You'll need a repairman too, though."

"Nope. No repairman. Not even you, Zach. You're going to get a vacation." Drew sighed, and turned to Zach, "I have some news, and I wanted to try it out on you before I told the rest of the employees. That's why I wanted you to come today. Not for clean-up."

Zach blinked, confused, "Am I gonna get fired?"

"No, but I won't stop you from quitting." Drew closed his eyes, "My wife... don't get me wrong, she's wonderful, but she wants... she's never liked the pet shop, you see. She's always wanted something less dirty, more modern... profitable. A pet shop isn't anything like that. What she really wants is... a computer store."

Drew closed his eyes for a second. Those few sentences had been hard, halting and somewhat mumbled. He tried to do better as he continued, "One with computers, printers, TVs, cell phones, music, videos... you know. And there isn't

one anywhere close. I mean besides that computer repair shop in the next town, but they don't sell anything… So she thinks it might be a good idea."

Zach shrugged, "It'd be easier to clean, sure."

Drew smiled politely. *Way to be, Zach. Should have expected that.* He tried to keep the grin on his face as he said, softly, "It makes sense, all in all. There's even a pet shop opening about thirty miles from here, so it's not like anyone won't have a place to get food. And my wife even said we could maybe put a side addition to keep selling food, just not the animals… she's allergic to fur. I don't know what I was thinking with the pet store in the first place. Uh, it's just… I liked animals. I even liked Glossy… but now…" He looked around. They were all gone, either they had run or they were fish, and therefore dead. It was going to take a while to get them back, if ever.

"You okay?" Zach said.

"Fine!" Drew said, a little too quickly and with a cracked voice. He felt horribly embarrassed, and was glad he could get this out on Zach before the adult employees. He had made sure Zach came early for that very reason. Zach was the first employee to set foot in the store for days. Even with the breathing room Drew had given himself, he still felt horribly worried. That was what Zach was for. Zach would feel too embarrassed himself to tell anybody else about Drew's nervousness. Drew needed that practice. He needed a lot.

He needed to rebuild everything from the ground up. To start over.

That was something he wasn't sure he had the strength for. He had even worn his uniform today, a polo shirt with the pet shop logo embroidered on it. It was a kind of denial, almost a hope that he could walk in and it would all be fine, he could go to work like every other day. That denial hadn't lasted long.

Drew sighed, deciding he was done, "Thanks, Zach. That's all I needed. I just wanted you to know what was going on. Once we fix everything, I'm going to need you to help us stock the store. And we might need some cleaning before then. I'll call you."

"Right!" Zach said. Never the one for a polite exit, he headed for the door, dropping his mop by an overturned cash register.

Drew couldn't take it.

"Zach, do you have a moment?"

"What?" Zach stopped, looking back.

"Would you…" Drew tried to figure out how to phrase it. He motioned with a finger. "Come here."

Zach hadn't even stopped walking before Drew began, "Would you think I was crazy, or seeing things or something, if I told you that on the night of the storm… I saw Glossy out on the road?"

"Nah." Zach said. When Drew kept looking at him, Zach added, "You're an animal man, Mr. Howell. The animals love ya. I wouldn't think it was weird if Glossy waved you goodbye before he ran for the hills!" He stuck his hands in his pockets in the characteristic lean, like the tower of Pisa about to tip, but never quite there, "Those animals are smart, Mr. Howell. I've seen it, and I know you have too."

"Thanks, Zach." Drew said, motioning for him to leave. Zach shouted something as he ran out the door and jumped onto the waiting skateboard, but Drew wasn't listening.

He was thinking. Thinking about what he had seen, the thing his wife wouldn't believe but he could swear was true. Sure, animals ran away, but that wasn't Glossy's way and he

hadn't told Zach what he had told his wife. How he could have sworn that *that* bunny had jumped in front of the bat, maybe even *dragged* him out of the path of the tires. Drew would have hit that bat. He had been sliding on the road, completely out of control. He would have hit him! Glossy, Drew knew, had saved that bat.

Animals didn't behave that way. No animal ever showed near that intelligence, thought that fast. And Glossy?

How could the only animal on the planet without a soul care for another?

Drew sighed, shaking his head and telling himself to forget about it. After all, whether he liked it or not, he was done with animals. Especially Glossy.

CHAPTER 5

"I don't know what the price of my life is, but I do know I'll never be able to repay it. I have to try, though."

–Arlen

Arlen had a dark secret, one he kept in the middle of the day. Day was the most secret time for a bat. Day was night and night was day, so a secret in the day was one the other bats wouldn't see. A night secret.

Instead of sleeping in Darkdoor, like he was supposed to, he was out in the sun for the fifth time since the storm. Arlen was going to go down to Haven, what the bunnies called their caves. Arlen pulled on the cloth stretched over his eyes and squawked softly, not wanting to wake anyone. They were drifting off into sleep in the perfect cave, Darkdoor, high above the waterfalls, overlooking Waterlog and Helaman Valley.

Squeaking again, Arlen checked the layout of the cave to make sure no more bats were flying. All of them were roosting, either taking refuge in tiny fissures in the walls, or just going straight to the ceiling and finding holds on the rock surface with their tiny claws. Most were asleep, but there was still enough movement that his exit wouldn't be noticed. Still, if he was seen, if Fallon or one of Fallon's buddies saw him leave... The results would not be pretty.

But he couldn't hesitate.

He let go of the ceiling, opening his wings. His body folded around in utmost precision, instinct kicking in as his wings grabbed the air and forced it underneath. That's how he had been taught. Shove the air under you, and jump off of it. It was a lot harder than that, but he didn't think of each step. And that was good, because now that he couldn't see, he would have a hard time learning.

Arlen longed for sight. He longed to be able to rip off the bandage covering his eyes, the scrap that had been scavenged from town, and look straight at the sun. It would hurt, sure, but it would be welcome pain. Glorious light. Oh sure, it wasn't like a bat had to ever use sight, not with echolocation, but it was like saying you didn't need any feeling in your chest because you didn't hold anything with it. Weird and discomforting. Now he had to tell when it was night and when it was day by feeling the sun, which meant he had no idea in Darkdoor. Arlen, though, didn't have a choice. Not since the storm. The wind had grabbed him, taking its revenge for being used by generations of his ancestors and throwing him into lightning. The other bats said it was a human string, but Arlen knew it wasn't. It was lightning, strings of lightning flashing through the air. Strings and strings of burning lightning.

Lightning hurt.

How had he survived? He should have died from it. The bats said he was almost run over too, but someone, some *bunny*, had rescued him.

Arlen circled in the dawning light, and let out a hard squeak. He saw the outlines of water, the shimmering confusion of reflections off the chaotic surface. Sprays in the air as it cascaded down the canyon, dead logs across the river forming

dozens and dozens of bridges.

This was Waterlog, water flowing down until it came to the humans. It was a good thing that humans stayed down there at the base of the canyon. The cars fenced them in on one side, and the canyon on the other. Otherwise, who knew how far they would spread? Like the cars, racing towards the horizon. At least humans weren't that strong, or that fast. If a human was as strong as a car… Arlen shuddered, only being thankful that wasn't the case, and squeaking again to mark his position.

Wind buffeted him, and he fought to right himself, grunting as the wind blasted the cloth across his face and knocked him off balance. He couldn't stop now, though. It didn't matter how tired he was, or how the sun blazed on his weak skin. The air smelled warm, humidity rising from the river.

He had to get to his place, his secret. That bunny that was always in the same spot, day after day. Oh, everyone knew a little about what had happened, but nobody knew quite as well as Lysander. The one with his head always tucked into the cold morning ground to cool the fire inside. The lightning. Arlen knew him by his small body, and the rough patch he had felt once on his head. It had the burned, fried feeling that had taken the place of Arlen's eyes. It was also obvious by looking at Lysander that he hurt on the inside too. Arlen knew it was probably just as bad, if not worse. Worst of all, was that it was Arlen's fault. He had been the reason Lysander risked himself and got hurt so horribly.

Arlen, squeaking, finally saw him. He was in his normal place, right outside Haven, sitting on that little perch just above a waterfall, and staring at the city. If Arlen wasn't out at night, where he saw the perch empty, he might have thought

Lysander never left.

Arlen landed. "Cold night, huh?"

"Cold morning." Lysander corrected. He was staring at the rim of sun peeking above the clouds. It was getting to where it couldn't be looked at. Arlen didn't see anything, though. He could only feel the thin ribbon of heat on his chest, from a sun not quite out yet. Echolocation didn't tell him about the sun. He saw it though, saw it in his mind and memories, and could swear he felt the warm glow.

Arlen got on all fours, squeaked to locate Lysander's face and looked at him. "Today?"

"Not today."

Arlen smiled and got up, "*Cheep!* Well, anytime, you know that, okay? Okay." He shook his wings, loosening them up before he went flying again. He turned towards Darkdoor, flexing his wings and preparing to go home.

That is, until Lysander added, "Soon."

Arlen felt the lightning run up his back again, and turned. "Soon?"

"Maybe soon." Lysander said. He was silent for a second, and Arlen wished his squeaks could let him see more than just the outline of Lysander's face, let him see what was going on inside his head as well. Not knowing was sometimes too much, especially when it came to this. Arlen, as horrible as it sounded, wasn't so sure about Lysander. Something was so very wrong about him. His voice didn't have any emotion. He kept far too still for a bunny. Bunnies hopped, jumped, and cowered. They didn't rest their head on a rock all day, staring into space. He was very odd.

"Did you know," Lysander's voice interrupted Arlen's thoughts, "That the cars, the things on those flat paths, aren't alive?"

If Arlen had an eyebrow, he would have raised it in skepticism, "They move."

"But they aren't alive, they're… things." Lysander's voice was hesitant, "I don't know what they are, but they aren't… they can't be animals."

Arlen cocked his head, wondering if he was hearing right, "You can't *chee!*, think that. They *cheerk*, move." He was squeaking in the middle of his sentences now. He did that when he got nervous. But Lysander had turned to look at him.

"The humans control them. They use them."

"*Chee!* The humans have nothing to do with cars!" Arlen said, squeaking like a bad case of hiccups.

"I saw one." Lysander said.

He was silent after that, and Arlen squeaked in frustration, "Saw a what? *Chee-ee!*"

"A human get into a car."

Arlen felt his brain skip a step, and he tripped backward, landing against a log, "Cars eat humans? Cars eat humans… *Ch-chirk…*"

"They don't—" Lysander said, but Arlen couldn't make out his words.

He was squeaking like crazy, "*Chee-chee-chee-chee—*"

"The humans use the cars!" Lysander said, raising his voice. The fact that he was actually showing emotion for once silenced Arlen immediately. It was the first time Arlen had been visiting that Lysander's voice had shown anything.

Lysander took a breath, his voice returning to normal, "The human that got in the car got out after the car stopped at another one of those places they live in." Lysander said coolly, "And if you watch, they do that all the time. And the humans

bring the cars to those things near the big road, and I think they feed them big ropes…" Lysander paused, "I think that the humans are in charge of the cars. The cars are forced to carry them places, and the cars have to wait until another human gets in them." Lysander said.

"But the cars on the big road don't have humans!" Arlen argued. He squeaked.

"They do." Lysander argued. "They just don't always stop here. I think that they carry the humans… somewhere else."

"Where else?"

"Maybe the humans live in different places." Lysander said. "They must live in two other places, since the road goes two ways."

Arlen's brain felt like it was being fried, just like Lysander's. "I don't get it… the cars carry the humans, but they… they aren't alive? *Chir?*"

"When they're not carrying a human, they're dead. No sound, no movement, nothing."

"But they're all like that at night, *cheep.*" Arlen said. "They're sleeping."

"No, the humans are, and so they aren't carrying them." Lysander said. "The cars are dead, and the humans make them alive."

"*Chrik!*" Arlen shook his head, "So what *is* a car?"

Lysander turned, or at least he was looking towards the town next time Arlen squeaked. "I don't know. But when I find out… that's when *soon* is going to be."

Arlen didn't understand a word Lysander was saying. He decided that for now, he didn't need to know. It was time to get home to Darkdoor. He squeaked, "See you then, *chirk!*" and took off. He squeaked a few times, and adjusted his course for the caves, feeling the hot sun begin to shimmer on his back. He was confused, and scared. Because if there was one thing he knew now, that he couldn't have even guessed beforehand, was the fact that Lysander wasn't just odd, but crazy. Completely crazy.

CHAPTER 6

"Just because no one had any idea what I was doing didn't stop me from doing it. After all, I had no idea myself."

–Lysander

Two weeks after the wind storm, Lysander went into action.

Mirada and the bunnies were hopping in for the night, scurrying and scanning for predators before entering the hole. It was the very end of dusk, so it was time to come in. Mirada and the rest of the bunnies made a habit to only look for food during the dusk and dawn, if possible. Daytime was too hot, and had predators. Night had even more predators than day. The best way to avoid it was to be outside in the in-between times, where most predators didn't care to look in.

Crickets were chirping, rather quickly, which meant it was going to be a rather hot night. Of course, any animal could feel that already, it had been such a hot day in the first place. It was the kind of day where the plants were as dry and brittle as the cracked earth. In the forest, the already crackly grass seemed to crisp and fry under the sun, the trees' dusty bark peeling off in layered sheets.

"He', Mira'a!" A bunny said, hopping up to her. Yerdle, or something. He held a half-bitten strawberry in his mouth. It

was so green it probably tasted awful. He grinned through the strawberry juice, "Wan' a bi'e?"

"No, Yerdle." Mirada said. She looked around, wondering. Something was a little different.

Yerdle spat out the strawberry, not even attempting to eat the thing himself, "Well, I have some roots back at my cave if you want to—"

"No." Mirada stated. She did it as a reflex. She was asked things like this so many times she had just grown accustomed to expecting it from anyone who talked to her. That is, everyone but Lysander. He wasn't like any bunny. That attracted Mirada, and made her more than a little curious.

"Okay." Yerdle said, put out, "Just... if you change your mind..." He hopped off slowly, head down.

Mirada turned, her fluffy large bulk scattering earth as she raised her head and sniffed. She looked to the point outside the hole, just above a waterfall. Lysander was gone from his resting spot.

Mirada sniffed deeply. Her nose, so used to finding food, met a chaotic mass of bunny smells. Most of them she knew by name, and the rest were somewhat familiar. She sought through them, wondering if maybe... yes, there it was. Lysander's smell was coming from inside the cave.

Mirada began to sprint for the tunnel, but just as quickly braked, tripping over herself and landing face down in the dirt. She had suddenly realized what a mess she was. A fine layer of dust covered her, mud caked on her paws.

She did a quick cleaning.

She sniffed herself, nearly panicked, and headed to the river for a wash. Did she smell nice? Maybe, maybe not. Now she smelled like moss from the river. But at least she wasn't

dirty, at least not too much. Mirada wondered if she should risk going and rolling in the flowers downstream, but there wasn't enough time. Mirada shook herself once and bounded for the hole, now the last one to get in. A few stragglers were still out there, but mostly everyone was here, shoving their way into the caves. Mirada was careful not to touch the dirty walls of the cave as she sniffed again, marking the paths Lysander had taken. She was always hitting the walls. The caves had all been built for smaller bunnies, not her. They were made for bunnies like Lysander.

Why had he gone inside so soon? It wasn't like him; he sometimes stayed out even at nighttime, despite the desperate warnings of others.

Mirada shook herself once outside a small room, the one given to bunnies not expected to live long, and peeked inside, "Lysander?"

Lysander was staring at the wall, and didn't move.

Mirada hopped inside, "Hot night." She noticed something had been scratched into the wall. It had been smoothed, and lines were drawn all across it. They must have been deep for Mirada to see them, because the light was fading rapidly, and only a sliver got this far in the cave. Lysander was covered in dust. He smelled like grass roots and crusted dirt, not altogether a bad smell. His dusty fur shimmered uneasily in the slivers of light.

"Mirada!" someone said behind her. She whipped around, smacking the wall and getting dust all over her coat. Mirada sniffed to figure out who was next to her. The smell hit her like a wall of dead fish.

"Tysell," She hissed, "Go! Go away!"

"He's been like tha' a' day." Tysell said. Her thin body,

rough and scratchy like her throaty voice, squeezed past Mirada to look at Lysander, "Staring at tha' wall, scratchin' in weir' ways…"

"I'm trying to talk to him!" Mirada whispered in near panic. How could Tysell talk that way about Lysander? What if Lysander thought Mirada was the same? He probably would! Mirada was feeling alarmed. He would hate her. And she hadn't even had an actual conversation with him yet.

Of course, Mirada could have expected that from Tysell. She actually liked Tysell. The bunny was very honest and open, willing to lay everything on the table at a moments notice. But she could also be blunter than a car hood slamming into a hillside. Tysell was useless at many things, including food gathering. She depended on Mirada to help her find food, and Mirada was sure to always be there. In return, Tysell kept off other bunnies wanting to cozy up to Mirada and was a shoulder to lean on when Mirada got emotional.

Which was often.

Today, though, Tysell was proving to be more of a hindrance than anything. Mirada shoved Tysell back into the hallway with her head, "Make yourself useful and get Lysander some food!"

"We're s'pposed ta be saving for winter!" Tysell hissed. "If he wants supper, he can get it himself! An' you don't have ta bail him out a' the time, no matta how much ya fancy him!"

"Tysell!" Mirada hissed, shoving her, "Sh! He might hear you!"

Tysell was frustrated, but not ready to give up, "Why you fancy him, anyway?"

"He's different." Mirada said, "I've been living my whole life in this place with a million faces, all look the same. He

doesn't look the same. Sure, on the outside maybe, but you can see… that he sees… different. You know?"

"No."

"He's from the humans, too." Mirada said, "Like me. He understands. You wouldn't."

Tysell shook her head, frustrated. "Figure not." She turned tail and left, kicking dirt in Mirada's face.

Mirada looked behind her at her now dirt-covered bulk, and wondered if Lysander had heard everything. Of course he had.

Mirada wanted to cry.

But no, she was in too deep now. She had to try and repair the damage, even if it was impossible. She turned to Lysander, who hadn't moved. "Sorry about Tysell. She's a little rude."

Lysander remained motionless.

Mirada inched closer, trying to resist cleaning herself, "You're foreign, right? You have a different voice, and you look… um… My parents used to be pets, but they escaped." Mirada hesitated, waiting for a reaction. She asked, "Did you… parents?"

Lysander was silent.

Mirada opened her mouth to fill the silence with something, anything. Before she could, that voice as smooth as his fur whispered, "I don't remember."

Mirada could have killed herself. "Oh… sorry."

"They aren't dead." Lysander said, "I think… sold, I think."

That didn't make Mirada feel any better, "What's sold mean?"

"Well, I used to live in a pet shop…" Lysander paused, "Never mind."

"What are you doing?" Mirada asked, trying to change the subject before she was even more rude.

Lysander actually looked over at her, though he certainly couldn't see her in the light very well, as huge as she was. He sniffed, "Thinking."

"About what?"

Lysander turned away. "Humans."

Mirada had already opened her mouth to say something, but the words caught in her throat, "H-Humans?"

"And… and things." He said, "Weird things. I don't know how to explain it."

"What's weird?" Mirada asked.

"Did you know that humans control other things?"

"Yeah." Mirada said, nodding as she picked up on the topic, "My parents used to live in a cage, and there was this dog that they had on a loud, metal string—"

"Not animals." Lysander said, "Things that aren't alive. It's like the cars, and some other things that move like cars… I can't see very well from up here, but they… they aren't alive, and the humans control them… never mind." Lysander moved to the wall, rubbing a paw over it, "But those lines stretched between poles that the humans put up… I think I figured it out. I think that's what makes everything go without being alive."

"What?"

"The lines!" Lysander tried to motion with his paw, but Mirada didn't know what he was pointing at, "They go to every single place of the humans, the places that light up at night! And you know what's in them? I didn't. But then, well… one hit me."

Mirada didn't know what to say, her mouth open in stunned silence, her brain locked in place.

"Lightning." Lysander said, his voice going so deep it scared Mirada. She hadn't known a bunny's voice could go that low, "Lightning is in the big lines, and that's why all the places are lit up. The lightning is going into the places."

Mirada blinked in confusion, "Why? How?"

"I don't know." Lysander said, "All I know is that they created it, they're the ones who made it so the lightning was in those lines, the ones that hit me. And that car that almost hit me is theirs too. I don't know how they work yet. But I'll find out, don't worry."

Mirada was confused, and a little scared by Lysander's tone. It was so dark, and yet had that same silkiness just like his perfect fur… She shook her head, trying to think of something to say. She had to say something.

But she couldn't think of anything. The silence grew longer. Lysander brooded against the wall, and Mirada realized that she was taking up almost all of the room. She began to turn, rubbing on all the walls, "Well… Lysander… bye, I guess."

"Bye."

That was it? Just 'bye'? Mirada felt crushed. Had she gotten nowhere? She realized for the first time that the conversation had been one-sided. He hadn't asked her anything; using her as an information dump.

Mirada began to slowly hop away, head down and ears back.

Lysander said, "Wait."

Mirada's heart thrilled, and she turned. "Yes, Lysander?" She was impressed how even her voice was.

"What's your name? I forgot."

"M-mrada, I mean, Mirda— Mordidida…. Miradidio…" She grimaced, "Mirarara…" She quit, hating herself. So much

for a steady voice.

"Bye, Mira." Lysander said.

"Bye!" She said, and skedaddled.

CHAPTER 7

"I used to be able to choose between right and wrong. Now I just have to pick the choice that's the least wrong."

–Arlen

The robbery was staged the night before the grand opening of Drew's new computer store.

That was about a month after the storm, with fall leaves coating the town in a blanket of red. The dim interior smelled of plastic and ink. It was as cold and silent as a graveyard, dead electronics lining the walls like a morgue. One computer had been left on, and was silently cycling through a demonstration movie. Soft beeps and chimes came from sleeping computers throughout the shop. The new security system was in, and fully operational, the cameras pointing in every direction over the rows of gleaming computers, printers, software, and accessories. They recorded everything, every move made by the two burglars as they went about their work.

First, thuds above the ceiling. Through the thin tiling, there was the sound of thumping, thumping. Then, the sound of scratching. One of the tiles began to crack. Something began to whack it repeatedly, and a piece broke off, clattering on the spotless tile floor. A few more pieces fell, the cheap tiling not meant to stand up to any forces, even the tiny thumps.

None of the cameras were pointed at the ceiling. Instead they pointed at the ground where a burglar was supposed to be. They didn't see the growing hole, only the tile pieces as they came down like snow.

Once there was a small pile of debris, the noise stopped. There was the flutter of wings, and something flashed past the cameras. That something screeched, the low noise registering on the cameras in the highest pitch.

"Lysander! *Cheerk!*" came a voice, "Where is it?"

"To the right… forward. There, that box."

A thick string descended from the ceiling. The shape flew back, squeaking and grabbing the string before flying back to the box Lysander had directed him to. Arlen tied the string around the box, no idea what was going on but not liking it one bit. One thing was certain: you did not mess with the humans, let alone take things from them. And what use did Lysander have for this box? Arlen had been expecting something in the months that he had known Lysander, waiting for the call to come, but nothing like this.

Arlen finished looping the string through a strap on the box, and flew back with the free end. Lysander was waiting in the roof, a rock sitting by him that he had used to punch a hole in the tile, and a 'screwdriver' that they had stolen from a 'garage' the night before. Arlen had no idea what those words meant, but Lysander insisted that's what they were called. They had to unscrew an 'air vent' so they could get inside the ceiling. It had been really hard to get that screwdriver working. Arlen hadn't thought it would work at all. Lysander, though, hissed that it *would* work. He had held the screwdriver in his teeth, wrenching his entire body around to get enough force to twist. Finally they had opened up the hole in the wall and entered.

Lysander took the string from Arlen in his teeth and began to do something weird with it. Arlen squeaked, but couldn't figure it out, "What are you doing?"

"Tying a knot."

"Did you learn that in one of the... books?" Arlen asked, the word foreign to him.

"Yeah." Lysander said, finishing the knot and pulling hard with his teeth to tighten it. Arlen watched as Lysander repeated the motion, chirping as softly as he could. He kept readjusting his bandages. Humans might be near, which terrified him. Not that Lysander cared. He wasn't scared of humans at all, claimed that most of them wouldn't touch him without a car, and he was safe as long as he made sure the roads were clear. He had actually been visiting the town.

Arlen thought Lysander was insane, or maybe really brave. He hadn't died yet, that was one good thing. He would sometimes be gone for so long, though. He was apparently 'reading books', full of 'pages', by using a broken air vent and sneaking into a 'library'. What on Earth was a library supposed to be? Whatever it was, Lysander had been at it every night for nearly a month, getting weirder and weirder the entire time. Arlen had wondered how Lysander could avoid predators on all of his nightly excursions. According to Lysander, he stayed near the road, where no animals came. Arlen wondered how he avoided the cars, but Lysander said that wasn't too hard.

He seemed so freaky now, reacting to questions long after they were given, or staring into space for hours on end. He claimed he was thinking, but would never say what he thought about. Arlen could only guess at what the other bunnies thought of him. He had never seen Lysander and other bunnies together, minus one girl bunny called Mirada. Maybe most of them were avoiding him.

Lysander headed up the air vent without a word, Arlen following. They had to get out through another opening out the side, through a piece of the air vent with a fan. Lysander stuck the screwdriver in; stopping the fan and making it groan and whine like an angry beast. Arlen went through the gap as fast as he could, hating every moment. Lysander told him the fan wouldn't hurt them, but Arlen doubted that. Any animal you provoked like that screamed and whined in fury, and was bound to hurt you sooner or later. Arlen just wanted to get out of there before it escaped and went after them.

Lysander and Arlen grabbed the string, and began to pull. Lysander bit it with his teeth, the knot stopping the string from slipping out. Arlen grabbed another knot with his claws. It was easy at first, until the box reached the point where it had to be pulled up. Then it took everything they had. Lysander pulled as hard as he could, his heart straining and reminding him of that day he had been so panicked before. He narrowed his eyes and pulled harder, feeling his spine bend under the stress and his neck burn.

Then, his body snapped backwards as the string went completely slack. It had snapped. There was the sound through the vent of something shattering.

An alarm blared.

Arlen gasped, reeling and clutching his ears, "*Cheet! Ch-chir!*"

"C'mon!" Lysander yelled, grabbing Arlen by his wing and yanking him toward the vent.

Arlen resisted, trying to get away, "I'm out of here!"

"I need that box!" Lysander said, "I can't get it by myself!" He was panicked now, not sure what to do. It was obvious that

he hadn't expected anything like this, no matter how much he read.

Arlen stopped, looking back, "But —*eep!*— what if humans come? With those loud sticks!"

"They're called guns!" Lysander said, "And I won't let them get us, Arlen. But I need you to help me!"

"What's so important about that box?" Arlen demanded.

Lysander opened his mouth to respond, but hesitated. Then, he finally said, "I want… I want them to see what their things can do. I want to show them that all those cars, and power lines, and computers, are doing… I want… I want them to feel what I did." Lysander rubbed the black stripe on his head, rough to the touch, and shuddered.

Arlen shook his head, not comprehending, "Revenge?"

"Not revenge!" Lysander said, "I'm going to teach them a lesson." He straightened, feeling the alarm strengthen him, each blaring noise a beat of his tiny heart, fast and high, "Those humans care nothing for any animal!"

Arlen shook his head fast, squeaking, "*Eep*… no, *cheerk!* Lysander, I… I care. You plan something bad to happen, you want to hurt them, right? Right?"

"Before, I was a robot! I felt nothing… here," Lysander rubbed his black stripe on his ear, "This has made me learn, made me feel! I think, now. I can actually do things, I'm not like before. I'm going to help the humans be like me."

"Like you…?" Arlen backed up, "I can't, I just can't help you." He heard more sirens in the distance. Car headlights approached and lights were blinking on, "I'm… I'm scared, *chirk!*"

"Arlen!" Lysander rose as high as he could, which wasn't very high. It had all been going so well, and now it threatened

to slip through his fingers. He couldn't let go now, he couldn't go back to where he was. So he pulled out his last card. He only had one thing left that could possibly work, and as horrible as it was, he used it:

"You owe me."

Arlen turned, looked back, "Don't say that."

Lysander stared back, "Arlen, I'm not asking. I'm telling you, help me. I can't fly, I can't see in the dark in there very well. You have to help me."

"No." Arlen stated, more of a question than a statement.

"I need you." Lysander said, "I need you like you needed me at that storm. You can't understand, I know. I promise this is for a good reason, Arlen. It's scary, it's dangerous, but I have to do it. I need to figure this out, and I need that box to do it."

Arlen gulped, shivered in the cold air. He was confused, unsure, but he knew he had no choice. He had to trust Lysander. Arlen chirped and nodded once.

"C'mon!" Lysander bolted down the hole. They arrived at the ceiling hole with the siren coming through it full blast.

Arlen groaned, slumping on a wall, "Too loud…"

"Go, c'mon!" Lysander said, grabbing an extra string he had, and shoving it at Arlen, "Go!"

Arlen stumbled out of the opening, and for a second Lysander thought he would smash into the ground. He flipped around ungracefully, finally finding his balance and flapping hard to slow his fall. He hit the ground next to the box, which had landed on a glass display case and smashed through.

Please don't be broken. Lysander thought as he watched above.

Arlen had the rope around the box again just as a screaming cop car streaked up to the entrance. Arlen flapped, con-

fused by the noise, and managed to get up to the air duct.

They pulled the box as they ran through the duct, Lysander grabbing the cord and letting his weight drag it up as he fell down a vertical shaft to the outside hole. There were shouts inside the store, and Lysander got the feeling they were going to be after them in a few seconds.

"Move!" Lysander yelled, to Arlen, and they dragged the box into a bush. Lysander pooled the cord under with them as two cops turned the corner. The lights blinded him, actually hurting as they blurred past. The two humans said something to each other, and got back in the car, zooming off into the night. Probably trying to chase down whoever had robbed the store, Lysander guessed. They had no idea. After all, an animal never messed with humans, especially not like this. They just assumed they were that powerful, but it hadn't worked this time.

Lysander was already planning his next move.

"Well… chee." Arlen was squeaking slower, "*Chir*— I— *chee*… I'm going."

"Not yet!" Lysander said.

"What?"

"I need a few more boxes."

CHAPTER 8

*"I grew up on the inside looking out at others.
Later, I made them look at me."*

–Lysander

The cord began at a small forest ranger station, and trailed on, and on, and on. Extension cord after extension cord were strung out, half buried in the dirt, hiding beneath bushes. It worked against the mudslide of the town, working up into the canyon. All the way until it rose into Waterlog.

The summer's heat beat down, never surrendering, but it had little effect on the single cord. It just kept on going and going, extension cord after extension cord for nearly a mile. People were going to wonder for a long time about the disappearance of so many cords, but no one would never think to look in the woods, and so the cords would ever be found. In time, they would be covered by a short layer of dead leaves and dirt, making them even more invisible than before.

The cord disappeared into a tiny hole, a short distance from Haven and all the other bunnies. Those bunnies stared at the hole, anxious and somewhat scared. Lysander's hole. He had dug it by himself in the side of the hill, overlooking the river. It didn't connect to the other tunnels, just a solitary world. It wasn't too different for a bunny to be by himself, of course,

but it was just another thing. One of those things in the pile of weirdness Lysander had brought from whatever place he came.

Lysander wouldn't make it long by himself, they said. They talked about how he wasn't natural, that the humans had messed with him and a predator was going to get him any day. They talked long into the night of how the loner, the straggler, was surely going to be the first to go.

The day Lysander had dragged in the end of the cord, he made his first public announcement. He announced it loudly, so that all the gossiping voices in the other caves heard him, and came out to see what all the fuss was. They huddled around the cave entrances, though, just in case. It was the middle of the day, not a time to be outside.

"You probably want to know what this is," He said, "It's called a cord. I know you don't know what a cord is, and I can't really explain. But I will tell you one thing. If you chew on this, it will kill you. It is not a predator, but you *will* die."

A murmur ran through the crowd. Mirada stood in front, with Tysell that she had brought along with her. Tysell grunted, "Then how d'ya die, then?"

"This cord is… is a container." Lysander said, trying for words that a bunny could understand, "It contains lightning, and if you bite it… the lightning comes out, and kills you."

"Are you crazy?" Someone asked, "You can't bring lightning here! That's like… like…"

"Adopting a wolf pup. As your own." A thick black bunny, Darshep, said. Those around him nodded and muttered agreement, a thing that often happened when Darshep spoke, "A bunny doesn't help a predator, no way, no how." Darshep turned to the side for a moment, "Hello, Tysell. Wonderful morning, isn't it? Shame Lysander has to spoil it for all of us."

A huge crowd of bunnies was gathering, flocking over and filling the places that weren't too close to the water. Hearing Darshep, more were becoming brave enough to come outside. And then they saw who he was talking to, and called their friends. A group of bunnies gathered around Mirada, staring in admiration at her perfect fur and huge build, praying she would make eye contact. But the only person she could look at was Lysander.

"It's not a predator!" Lysander said.

Darshep stepped forward in an act of bravery not like a bunny. Lysander didn't back down, even when Darshep said, "So what is it?"

"It's a machine!"

Silence fell. Eyes turned to the new voice, Mirada.

Tysell nudged her. "What does *that* mean?"

"A machine is a lifeless beast!" Lysander yelled to the crowd, "A machine has no soul or heart, yet gives more power to those who control it than... than a thousand wolves! This cord has enough lightning, enough raw power, to burn a forest! Cars are the same way. A car is a machine! What animal can stand against a car?"

Darshep grunted, "So they *are* preda—"

"No!" Lysander cut across him, "A predator has a mind, a way of thinking, like us. A machine has no thoughts, no feelings. It does what it is told, and nothing more. It doesn't taste or smell or touch, but it obeys orders."

"Whose orders?" Tysell grunted, "Yours?"

"This cord obeys me, because I own it," Lysander said. "But most machines are controlled by something else."

"What?"

"Humans."

At Lysander's words, there was an absolute, total silence. The eyes of the bunny crowd were blank, not understanding. Or maybe they didn't want to understand.

Darshep took a few steps backward, "You're saying the humans control... all those things? The cars... and the lightning... and everything?"

"That's what I'm saying." Lysander said.

Darshep sneezed, shaking himself, "So a human can call down lightning? Storms as well?"

Lysander corrected him, "No, not storms. Just... lightning."

"Lightning without storms." Darshep said, "Well, I don't know where you think that thought came from, but that's just not true."

"It is true!" Lysander said, looking back and forth. Mirada would have thought he would be put off by all the opposition, but his face was only annoyed, as if they all were just stupid and couldn't understand him. She wondered if that was true.

Tysell snorted next to her, "So he really *is* crazy."

Darshep shook his head, black fur glistening, "Your brain has been turned to soup by that little accident of yours, and we want none of it. Normal bunnies don't act like you, you aren't one of us! You're just... odd. That's all I can call you, Lysander. Odd."

"Odd... odd..." The word went like a whisper around the crowd. They stared over each other, climbing on top of each other so they could have a better look. Their eyes were wide and bright, but their ears were down flat, terrified. The tense crowd buzzed like a beehive, always looking around, checking for predators. But they also kept a wary eye on Lysander. Lysander knew he was marked, but the thought didn't really register in his brain. That wasn't important right now, after all. The only thing that was important was the cord, it didn't matter what anyone else thought.

Lysander looked around once, and with a huff, dragged the cord into his cave. Inside, he shoved past the shredded, bitten apart remains of almost a dozen boxes, transparent plastic crackling under his feet. He shoved the cord into a power strip, other cords trailing from it, and poked the switch with his nose. It was a process he had learned from days of spying on humans, from learning their ways and hoping one day he could use them.

Lysander didn't understand what everyone's problem was. He couldn't believe no one understood. No one in a hundred or however many generations of living near humans had ever figured out what he had. Lysander opened the clasp, shoving his head into the crack of his stolen trophy, his prize, shoving it open. He looked for what he wanted, and poked it with his nose.

A glowing rectangle of light blasted the tiny cave, showing the new walls in blinding light. Lysander cringed, blinking and trying to adjust his eyes. It was like a miniature sun. The lightning was in there.

Lysander waited patiently as the screen began to do things. It flashed, squares and patterns forming across it. Something was happening inside. Lysander knew he had to wait. He knew that some machines, though they didn't seem to do much at first, had only to wait a little bit to see their true power.

And this was the most powerful kind. Lysander had looked, snuck into and surveyed the places that the humans went. Like the pet store, they gathered and exchanged green papers, or money, for items, food, and machines. And of all

the machines, the section with this kind, the kind of glowing rectangles and images, was the ones that they gathered around most, that they spent the longest time picking, and the ones where the most green was forked over. The importance was obvious, though Lysander didn't know why.

The screen had stopped moving. Lysander looked, deciphering the tiny symbols which, somehow, he was the only animal that understood. Besides humans.

Please type a username to begin setup.

Setup… to get ready. Yes, Lysander had seen that word before. And type, that meant use the keys. Type what? Username… A name? No, not exactly. But what did… oh, of course. User of the machine.

Press the keys, make the name of the one who used the machine.

Lysander leaned over the keyboard, about to press when he realized something.

He didn't know how to spell his name.

His spelling was impossible. He barely understood the words, let alone all the little orders and rules that he knew were there. How was he supposed to spell Lysander?

Maybe a different name, a simple one. That was what he needed. But what? What could he call himself? Lysander glanced behind at the now silent cave mouth. Someone was talking.

"Hey, Lysander?"

Mira. Or whatever her name was.

"I know that those guys can be kind of mean, but… you don't need to sulk! I brought you some carrots… I was supposed to save them for winter, but… I just thought…"

Lysander waited, not realizing the hesitant slant to her

voice, the yearning for an answer. His mind was blank, still thinking. Name… name…

"I'll just… leave them here, yes." Mira said, and there was a little scuffling, "Eat them before the bugs do! Okay… Lysander… I don't know. Those other bunnies think you're odd, but I don't! I don't think you're odd! Yeah… 'kay… Bye!"

She scampered off, but not without leaving an idea behind. One that Lysander caught. They thought he was odd, huh? They were right.

He turned back, and punched the three keys.

Odd.

Lysander pressed enter.

CHAPTER 9

"It's not something I learned. It's an instinct. I breathe electricity. I feel machines. I live on fire, not food. I am what humans wish they could be."

–Lysander

It had all begun, so long ago, with diapers.

Diapers was the first word Lysander had understood. The first human word he had read. He had been staring into Helaman Valley, looking, squinting. One sign by the highway, large and colorful, had caught his attention. It was a human, without clothes. A very young one, wearing nothing but a puffy white cloth around its legs. Lysander knew about clothes from the pet store. Humans wore different clothes each day, skins that could be taken on and off. Removable fur. On the sign by this human was the word, in bright white:

Diapers.

It was so far away Lysander could barely read it, but somehow he knew. He knew that the string of scribbling had to mean the white thing the human child wore.

After that, it came quickly.

He had watched, waited. The more he saw the more it made sense. Actions by the humans had meaning now. The cars were there for a reason, not just wild beasts. The roads were paths just for them. The humans actually *built* the giant boxes they lived in. Lysander found this information came easily. It seemed to snap together as easily as a twig could be broken.

It was the lightning.

Lysander could feel it in his head. It had a constant ache, but a good one. One that made him concentrate, that made things fuse together. Like a giant jigsaw puzzle. The human world was greater than anything Lysander knew. They had it all. There were no predators or prey. There were only the humans and what they allowed to live. He read and read, learning of fire and metal and weaponry and electricity. Ton upon ton of industry, humans surviving in places evolution never intended them to reach. They even could reach past the sky, to the moon and beyond.

"It hurts." Lysander had told Arlen. This had been before the robbery, before the computers. Before the plan.

"Sorry." Arlen said. He squeaked a few times, figuring out the darkness of the cave, and realized something, "Wait, what hurts?"

"Lightning." Lysander closed his eyes, "And it isn't… isn't in my head, you know? The pain. It's… in my stomach."

"Your scar is giving you a stomachache?"

Lysander shook his head, turning away from Arlen. He didn't know how to explain it. Arlen took a few steps forward, right at his side. As he did so, the pain got worse. Lysander suddenly thought of how he had treated Arlen. Something seemed wrong about that. He felt suddenly he shouldn't have been so demanding.

But why not?

"It's down here." Lysander prodded his own chest, "Right by my heart. It gets worse when I think of humans and the pet store. My throat clogs and my eyes get all wet so I can't see."

Arlen breathed in softly, "That isn't stomachache. That's heartache. Mom used to call it Black Fever."

"Black Fever?" Lysander said. The name sounded odd, but it made sense in a way.

"It's a panic sickness." Arlen said, "The more you fight it the worse it gets. And you can't cure it just by sitting around and waiting."

"How do I get rid of it?" Lysander said, "I'd do… *anything*. I need to feel better. That's all I need."

"Well… you have to know why you have it." Arlen said, "I got it when mom died. I was so sad and I almost panicked. I couldn't eat for almost a day and almost went into hibernation. In the summer."

Lysander blinked, "Your mom…"

"And dad." Arlen sighed, and cheeped softly, "I bet you know how that is. Heard you came from the human place. Not many bunnies there ever stay with parents."

Lysander was silent.

Arlen flapped, clinging to the roof of the tunnel. He knew it would unnerve Lysander, but Arlen was already queasy, and being right side up only made that worse.

"I can't remember." Lysander said.

Arlen nodded, "Bet that thought just made it hurt more."

Lysander agreed silently, and softly asked, "How did you fix it?"

"I didn't." Arlen said, "It was Fallon. He forced me to keep going, shouted at me until I started flying again. Wouldn't let me back in the cave unless I had eaten. After a while I could tell myself to keep going. Have to do it every day. I have to go out in the world that killed both my parents and pray it doesn't kill me too."

"I can't." Lysander said, voice cracking, "That's impossible. No one can do that. Not while thinking… about…"

"You can't think about that!" Arlen dropped from the roof of the cave, scrambling up to Lysander, "*Cheep!* Thinking makes it worse. You have to *do* something. Something that takes up every part of your mind and doesn't let you go back. I use what mom said. I be nice to everyone. That's impossible, see? You can't be nice to everyone. So I have no time to think about mom being gone. I don't have time to think about dad not there. Fallon does the same. He's leading the entire clan. No one's ever done that."

"So… I just have to find something. A direction."

Arlen nodded, squeaking, "Yes, —*eep!*— If you can't do anything but feed the pain, it won't do anything but grow."

"Then I won't." Lysander said, "Heartache. I won't listen to it. I'll ignore my heart and stomach and everything!" The very words seemed to fill him with strength. He could breathe easier.

"What'll you do?" Arlen asked, "You have to do something. At least at first. Something impossible. Then, when the pain goes… you're cured. You're free."

"Right." Lysander said, and thought, "I just realized something. It all started with them. They caused the Black Fever. To you, to me, to every animal in Waterlog and the entire planet!"

"Planet?"

"I'll stop it." Lysander said, "I'll fight it! I probably… can't. But I'll try. Nothing is harder than beating them."

"Beating who?"

"The humans, Arlen. The fire makers. The machinists. The great and powerful."

Lysander took a few steps, looking outside where there

was a bright white moon and a scattering of stars. Looking down, he saw the stars sprawled along below as well. Helaman Valley. The humans could even make their own stars.

Lysander planned to take them away.

CHAPTER 10

"They tell me we always want things that we can never have. Maybe that's why everyone tries to be so perfect. I want to be perfect."

–Mirada

Mirada was starting to doubt herself. She had used to be one of the best, not exactly perfect, but better than most other bunnies around. Enough so that other rabbits would try to impress her, try to get her to fall for them. But they were all so plain! Mirada didn't think she was being mean, at least she hoped not, but so many bunnies… they were like clones.

She was like a clone, too, of course. It was for survival. It was the techniques, handed down. The way of dodging, running, constantly checking for danger that had made Mirada survive. But everyone ran, dodged, checked for danger. They all did it, every day, without giving a single thought for tomorrow except maybe storing some food. It all seemed… trivial.

But Lysander wasn't like that! He hadn't grown up with all the others, like Mirada had. He stared blankly, and proudly hopped in the open like there wasn't any danger. If there was danger, he was oblivious to it. He stood out like a solid white star against the hurrying crowds of beige and black and brown. When she could get him to talk, he would tell her things, things about a liquid food for the cars, which belched putrid

air. Lightning that ran through cords and gave things light like the sun, but not being the sun, instead being those little square stars down in the town. Windows, he told her. Invisible, but hard. Every time he talked he told her something so different and amazing that she could only wonder at what he meant.

Like yesterday. Mirada had done something she shouldn't have. Every day, she tried to bring Lysander food. This meant that sometimes she didn't get to eat, but that was okay. Unfortunately, that day she hadn't been able to find food. It had been so dry lately the plants were becoming harder and harder to eat. Nobody had found anything except a few little grass roots, so dry they had to be soaked in the river for some time before eaten. So Mirada had borrowed, or rather stolen, food from the stores in the caves to bring him.

Of course, everyone could take food from the stores, but it wasn't a good thing to do. It had to be conserved for winter, all the bunnies were supposed to be adding to it, not taking away like she was. Besides that, Darshep had said that Lysander wasn't to get any food, since he hadn't helped gather. If he truly wanted to be by himself that was the way it had to be. And when Darshep said something like that, everyone was expected to listen. That was Darshep. There wasn't any exact leader of Haven. Nothing like that bat, Fallon, up in Darkdoor. If there was a leader, though, it was Darshep. He said something, and it was usually done. But that didn't mean Mirada couldn't disobey.

So Mirada had to sneak the food out, looking around corners of tunnel intersections, trying to sniff out bunnies ahead of her in the darkness. A few had talked to her, but she just said she wanted to eat outside, that's why she was dragging these plants. She wanted to see what she was eating. They let her through, though Mirada was sure that they had to be wondering why she had brought her food indoors only to drag it out again. They might even tell Darshep about it. Mirada gulped, and moved faster.

When Mirada made it to Lysander's cave, she tried to be as quiet as she could, not wanting to disturb him. But she didn't want to surprise him either, so she tried to be loud. But still quiet. Somewhere in the middle, loud enough to make him notice but not loud enough to be distracting. Then Mirada remembered she should have preened herself, but it was too late for that.

"Hi, Mira." Lysander said when she came in. She was momentarily blinded. The giant machine, trailing the cords that Lysander had warned everyone about, sprawled along the wall of a large cave. A glowing rectangle of light, like a giant square star, shimmered from it. Those tiny little marks on everything that the humans used were displayed in neat little rows along the screen. Lysander had once told her they contained words, messages that were, he said, *read*. A way of hearing someone talk with sight, not sound. The humans apparently spoke without talking, it would seem.

"Hi!" Mirada found herself saying after her eyes adjusted. But she had paused too long. It was already awkward. And it was her fault. She begged silently for Lysander to break the silence, to say something to her. She eventually followed with, "How's it going?"

"Good." Lysander said. The way he cut off so abruptly made it obvious he wasn't going to ask how *she* was. She scooted forward, "Here, I brought you these." She dumped the leaves on the machine.

"What the!—" Lysander looked around, his eyes wide

and completely terrified… or angry.

Lysander shoved her out of the way, frantically grabbing the leaves and heaving them to one side, "Mira! What do you think you're doing?"

Yep, he was angry. Mirada closed her eyes, trying to block it out. She shook a little.

"You can't get grime in the keyboard!" Lysander rubbed a paw back and forth across it. The little pieces jumped up and down, clacking and clicking like rain on a sleeping car, and more scribbles appeared on the screen. The thing even beeped, making Mirada jump. But she was too busy cowering to worry about that. She had fouled things up again.

"Is it bad?" She asked to Lysander, his eyes fixed on the keyboard.

"No." Lysander said. He sighed, turning and smacking down on the buttons with more force than before. He had to use one paw for each click. From the way he moved, Mirada could tell he was impatient.

"Lysander…?" Mirada prompted.

He didn't respond.

"Lysander, when you first came here… I didn't see you ever get sad or happy or anything. But now… Now you seem really angry. Why's that?"

"Why do you want to know?" Lysander asked, his voice unnaturally even.

Mirada tried to choose her words carefully, "I… I want to help."

Lysander clacked a few keys, and without turning, said, "You can't help, Mira. It's nice of you to offer, but you can't. Not unless you can beat the humans. If you can block their lightning, douse all the fires, stand in front of an automobile and stop it dead in its tracks… Or if you can outthink them. A bunny can't do that."

"You sound like they did something to you." Mirada said, "That's why, isn't it? Why you never seem to care. They did something horrible to you."

"Look, you can see." Lysander pointed to the black scar, the place of no hair and scorched skin, what he had seen reflected in glass and the dark screen of his own computer. Mirada stared at the scar. A black smudge that wouldn't wash away. She knew of course, that one of those long lines, the ones full of lightning, had hit Lysander there. He had survived, somehow, which showed just how amazing he was. What horrified her is that, judging from what Lysander had said, the humans had done it all on purpose.

She believed that.

Mirada said, "So you were different before then? You were a normal bunny?"

Lysander turned away, looking at his computer. Mirada didn't add anything, hoping that the silence would force an answer out of Lysander for once, instead of forcing another question from her. She wondered how long she could hold it.

Lysander moved forward, sticking a paw on top of the huge glowing screen. He pulled it down, folding it in half until it clicked loudly. The room was sheathed in a smoggy brown, almost too dark too see. Different colored lights bathed the room as they blinked. Red, orange, green, blue…. sometimes more than one. It was like Lysander's own set of shimmering, distant stars. It even gave the illusion that Mirada was outside, until she moved back and felt the cave wall against her.

Lysander's voice echoed in the room, "I was different. I didn't see as clearly. I think I was just like a normal bunny. The

lightning… I don't think it quite left me. It's just… you know how you can smell a thousand different things, and only one is something you can eat, but you still can find it, with all the other smells? It's like that… It was all big and confusing, and now it almost seems to sort itself! Now I understand writing, and human speech, and can even… um, yeah." He cut off, like he had been about to say something he shouldn't. Out of the dark, his voice began again, "But I wasn't normal. I haven't been normal for a long time."

"But you said that the lightning wire thingy only hit you back in the late summer! When we found you." Mirada said. Technically, it was they, not we, but Mirada decided it might be nice if Lysander thought she had helped in the rescue. It couldn't hurt.

"Then it had to have happened before the lightning, wouldn't it?" Lysander said.

"What happened?"

"The humans. They…" Lysander's words rattled in his throat, and he cut off, "Mira, just… just go."

"But I…" Mirada stopped, knowing that when Lysander made a decision, that was that. She murmured an apology and shuffled out as fast as she could.

Once again, Mirada had almost done something right. And then messed it up worse than it was to start.

CHAPTER
11

"I could care less about being brave, as long as I'm never afraid."

–Drew Howell

"Look, bub, it's broke. I need it fixed," the man said, slamming the box on the counter so hard that a leaning stack of papers collapsed, sliding all over the floor. The customer smirked, wiping a hairy arm over his nose and snorting, "You gonna clean that up?"

You need the cleaning. Drew thought, but didn't say it aloud. In fact, the very thought of saying it aloud made his knees quiver, his stomach cinching up into a clod of embarrassment. He crouched down, scooping up the papers with one hand. Manuals on every computer invented since electricity. The computer that the man shoved at him looked even older than that.

Drew gulped, holding the papers tightly to his chest as he got up, "Sir, I'm sorry, but the thing is that the model isn't under warranty anymore, and additionally they don't make parts for that make—"

"Parts? Who said anything about parts?" The man's eyebrows clenched into a single mass. He looked like the kind that would tear the head off of anyone who tried to con him.

And maybe those who didn't.

"Sir… just a moment." Drew shoved the papers under the counter, and pulled a keyboard towards him, "What you have is nearly ten years old, and it looks to me like the storm we had shorted out all the fuses. It would need a new power supply, which isn't made anymore."

"I don't want all this mumbo-jumbo magic techno talk!" The customer said, drawing circles with his finger in the air to demonstrate, "My daughter's teaching me to use the internet, that's all it needs to do."

"You don't know how to… sir, do you even have internet service?"

"Of course!" The man cocked his head, "Service?"

"Have you been paying an internet provider to—"

"No!" The customer yelled, "My daughter says everything on the internet is free. I'm not paying for anything."

"Not paying." Drew said. He turned away, resisting the urge to sigh in exasperation. After building up a certain amount of courage, he turned to the man, "As much as I want to, I can't fix this computer."

"You're the computer guys! Fix it! Fix it!" The man shoved the box across the counter and straight into Drew's chest. He caught it, grunting under the weight of the massive dinosaur.

Drew grimaced, "I… I… I'll see what I can do."

"Good." The customer grunted, and turned to leave, "And if you *dare* make me pay too much money, you'll be sorry."

He lumbered away, bulldozing through the glass doors so fast that they let out a low boom. Drew winced, wondering if they would shatter. On the glass, a sweaty handprint gleamed.

"You never could say 'no', could you?" Drew hissed to himself. He sighed, and adjusted the box so he could carry it

into the back room. He doubted there was hope for the fossil of a computer he held, but if he didn't try that man was sure to be even angrier than what Drew had just seen.

If that were possible.

Drew shoved through the door to the back rooms with a shoulder, dumping the box on a table with several others. He wondered if he should get the cleaning supplies and fix the handprint, but couldn't bring himself to do it. All he had energy to do was shuffle to his office and slump in his desk. He stared at the screen for a few minutes, and finally summoned enough conviction to check the e-mail.

Drew scrolled his mouse. There were maybe fifty e-mails from suppliers wanting him to stock their products. The problem was that he only stocked what he had already ordered before all the e-mails came, and so didn't have the shelf space for anything new. He began to delete them all in bulk. His computer at the office was so much better than his home one. His home computer would freeze up whenever he tried to turn on the internet, so he rarely used it. He actually had to go to the library if he wanted the internet at all. It was such a long shot from his college days, studying computer technology and business. He fondly remembered late night discussions with his friends about operating systems and programming issues, arguing as they sat around the lobby TV, video console plugged in and set on multiplayer.

Now he was back to computers, it seemed. Drew had mixed emotions, almost as mixed as his office. He really needed to organize, even if all he accomplished was clearing a path to the door. It would be better than wading through invoices and cardboard boxes every time he needed a restroom break. He was just used to clutter. At the pet shop it hadn't mattered so much, but here it was getting in the way. For now, Drew ignored that problem, just focusing on cleaning up his mail.

After glancing through the pile of spam on his computer, he turned to the paper mail. He usually looked at these, instead of the e-mails. If the message mattered, they usually sent it on paper. And the magazines were easier to read than constantly clicking through an online store. As he shuffled them, one caught his eye. First, it was the lack of a return address. Then he noticed it wasn't postmarked, not even a stamp. How had it gotten in with the rest of the mail? He fumbled in his desk until he found a broken pencil. He sharpened it and used the tip like a makeshift letter opener. Then he tossed the pencil aside, where it accumulated with all the other junk on his desk. A letter and a glimmering CD slid out onto the table.

Dear Mr. Howell,

First off, let me say. I'm the one who robbed your store place. It was wrong. I see it, it was the only way I get a computer. I cannot buy one. I am a very odd person. I do promise to pay back, in fact, I'll pay back a hundred dollars times over price of computer.

But I don't have that money right now. I can get it. But you must help. I can't do a lot of things, like get a job, make money. Life is not fair.

But you can do, you own store, have business knowing. I have an idea, and I can do it. It'll earn money. Lots of it. I make proposition. You to set up a website. I'll give you easy instructions, help a lot. You own website, and get every penny and quarters. That would pay you back.

You must be suspicious. But I'm not a bad guy and I'm not a

con artist. You are not lending me money, I'm giving. I ask is that you trust me. Follow my directions.

You probably wonder how website would make money, which is fair question. It would be selling something I make, hard to explain. I've attached a file on the CD for you.

You will understand.

Hoping for your acceptance,

Odd

The letter contained a single e-mail address on the bottom. Drew squinted, not believing a word. And yet… something was weird. It was probably just a virus in that CD, opening it would kill everything on the network. But why would a hacker personally target him? Was it because they had indeed robbed him, and now wanted another go at his store? Or was it something else, maybe not even a lie?

Drew knew what to do. He took the CD and carried it to the back room, where computers were being repaired. He opened a bin marked 'Recycling' and pulled out a laptop. It was going to be thrown away because it was so old it couldn't do anything. Except maybe check for a virus.

It took forever to boot, and even longer to get the CD on it. But when it did load, and Drew launched the program, the screen flickered, and slowly changed. Drew, eyes lidded from a long day at work, tapped at the computer. He was sick of this. He should have just stuck with the animals. Even trying to sell that one bunny was sometimes better than this. Besides that, the computer store wasn't working out as well as he hoped, and

he didn't have the motivation to try and figure out what was wrong.

Drew's pessimism vanished when he saw what was on the screen.

Experimentally, he clicked a few things. Then typed a little. Then, eyes growing wide, he realized what he was seeing.

Drew ejected the CD mid-program, not usually a smart thing, and sprinted for the store's biggest computer. This was going to need everything he could give it. Because if this is what he thought it was… Then maybe there was something to that letter after all. A big something.

CHAPTER 12

"He comes into our lives out of nowhere. And when he arrives, we believe he's a miracle, or something. I don't believe in miracles."

–Jessica Howell

After Drew accepted Odd's offer, the instructions came as fast as lightning.

Every order was precise, the instructions down to the letter, not a margin for error anywhere. The first problem Drew had was not being able to keep up. He would scarcely finish the instructions on one letter before the next one appeared somewhere. Maybe under his car's windshield wiper, or on his desk at work, or simply delivered in the morning mail. But they were never postmarked, and lacked a return address. Occasionally, it would come in his e-mail from an address that had already been deleted. Drew sent a few emails to the address Odd had given in the first letter, but there was no response or indication that he received them. Somehow, though, Odd always seemed to know if Drew was doing things the way he wanted.

Drew even had to take time off his job, throwing his duties on Zach and other employees in order to spend more and more time in the back room. All for Odd. A person he had never met, a person who had stolen from him and who he should certainly report to the police. But he did everything

Odd asked, hoping, wishing that together, he and Odd could make it work. It didn't matter that Odd refused to meet in person, that every little instruction had to be done by Drew, without Odd's hand in it at all.

In fact, it could be said that Drew had done it all.

Odd could simply disappear, and anyone who knew would say it had all been Drew. Drew had been thinking about that for a while, and it seemed that Odd knew too. He asked at least once per letter that Drew keep following his instructions, keep listening to him.

A lot of people would think he was nuts. Drew would have thought that too, but now that he knew what Odd had created, he had no hesitation at all.

"It's an *operating system*." Drew told his wife, "Downloads on any computer." He was following her around the kitchen, waving the disk through the air like a conductor's baton. He had backed it up in three places, like Odd asked, so the disc wasn't too important anymore. Jess was wiping down all the counters, cleaning off the spots that she always swore were there, though Drew couldn't see them anywhere. This kitchen was her fortress of cleanliness, her last stronghold against the mess of Drew and the kids. If you walked through the house, starting at the entertainment room downstairs and walking all the way to the kitchen on the other side of the house, the mess would seem to drain away, slowly disappear. Here in the kitchen, an almost visible aura of bleach and soap seemed to waft off of the chrome appliances.

She gave him a sideways look, "Drew, I told you I don't know anything about computers. You have to run the store."

Drew groaned, frustrated. He tried to explain that this wasn't a product at the store, tried to tell her the story.

That didn't work so well.

Jess threw down her towel, "What if this... this *Odd*, is a hacker or a terrorist or something? Odd can't be a real name! And you want to make a... a *business proposition* with him?"

"Look!" Drew said, gesturing to the laptop on the kitchen table, "I wouldn't normally... but this is amazing! This operating system is a hundred years past anything we have!"

"Why? What is an operating system, anyway?" She asked.

"Well... it's the heart of the computer. It's like a program, but it's in charge. It's the boss, makes everything on the computer run. The big computer companies, the kind that make computers and all of that? This is what it's all built on. And on top of that, there are very, very few types of operating systems currently being sold. Everyone makes programs, but nobody makes operating systems."

Jess turned to him, her face betraying her unbelief, "And this one is special, somehow?"

"I don't know why... but it... it goes faster. My computer is running as fast as it did when it was brand new, and on top of that... well, normally, certain programs only work with certain systems. This game works on this computer, this app works on this phone, if you want it for something different you're going to need to buy another copy of the program, built for that system. This thing, it runs all of them!

"You can download a program from anywhere, no matter what system, and it will work perfectly. Or better than perfectly, since it runs faster. It's like a phone and a laptop and a tablet, all in one. And when you start, you get to pick a color, and each color is a different way to run your computer! I'm using blue, since it's the simplest one. Red is good for speed, purple makes pictures and videos run so smooth and perfect... I think yellow is a sort of social network promoter, it has updates and things…"

"You've lost me."

Drew shook his head in frustration, leaning on the slick counter as he tried to find a way to put it. "Look. Think of it this way. This thing, you download it, and it all works. It goes faster, it works with everything, it never glitches, and it instantly personalizes to be the computer that you want it to be."

"That sounds…" Jess blinked, "It sounds like a scam. Whatever Odd told you, he must be lying. No computer does that."

"Odd didn't tell me anything. I've been figuring it out by myself. I've been working with the program, figuring out how it works."

"You've been programming it?"

"No, it's all locked up, but that's normal. That's standard security against viruses."

"Well…" Jess frowned, "Just… be careful, dear. Sometimes it's too good to be true. This Odd character may not be as perfect as you think."

But he *was* perfect. In less than a week, Odd's perfect instructions guided Drew through the steps. Opening accounts, hiring a website designer. A custom website, pretty as ever, was up in less time than Drew knew was possible, and for a quarter of the price he would have guessed. The site was a promotional site for the Triangle System, what Odd insisted that the operating system be called. *Why*, Drew asked in an e-mail.

Ask me again in a month, Odd replied.

He refused to talk about it. And so Drew didn't push. He didn't even attempt to ask why the company was named *Bunny Computers*, which certainly wouldn't have been first on Drew's list of names. Odd's instructions were done, and in less than a week, somebody had paid for a copy of the Triangle System. It was expensive, too, almost as expensive as current operating systems.

Despite that, people bought it. People began to come, more and more, funneled in by the special advertising system that Odd had told Drew to use. It was better than anything else, years beyond. In fact, it began to attract the attention of several big sites, news sites about technology.

One day, Drew got a call from one of them. He was in the computer shop, poking the insides of a computer with a metal pick and wondering how it had managed to light on fire. The things people could do to computers!

The phone was so loud he jumped. He grabbed it in a stranglehold, nearly stabbing himself with the pick, and finally answered, "Hello?"

"Hello. Name's Cory Yalk. Wondered if we could talk." The person on the line said, with a light Southern accent, "Are you Drew? Drew Howell?"

"Yes…?"

"I want to talk to you. About your… program. If it *is* a program. Honestly, I don't know what that is."

"Well, it's an operating system." Drew explained, "You download it on your computer and—"

"I know that! I have a copy, I bought one. What programming language did you use?"

"Programming? Why do you want to know?"

"I work for some of the biggest news companies ever. Sometimes, I have to figure out how things work, inside info, you know? But that operating system… I've been taking it apart, reverse engineering? It's unlike anything I've seen! I went

STEVEN OLSEN - 74

to school, learned everything they could teach me, but I never saw this. How does it work? I'm not trying to copy or anything, I just need it for my news stories. You know, basics. Why it runs faster, how it does that thing where any program works, no matter what the program is made for... how you got it to switch the way it functions, to resemble different systems. Who helped you make it?"

"Helped me? No one helped me!" Drew said, confused. Who was this guy, anyway?

"You did it all by *yourself?*" Cory's tone dripped disbelief, "Hah! Don't think so!"

"I didn't make it!" Drew said, his heart jumping instantly.

Odd's warning came back to him. *Don't ever reveal who made this. You made it. I don't exist.*

Cory was oddly silent, and finally said, his quiet voice cutting through Drew's confusion, "Maybe you should start at the beginning. Is this a bad time to do an interview?"

"No! No... it's just, I'm not sure how much I can say because Odd doesn't really want—"

"Hold on there... that didn't sound right. What's Odd? Is Odd a person?"

"Yes. I mean no! I mean... argh!" Drew pulled the phone away and smashed his head on the desk in frustration.

"What was that noise?" Cory asked.

"Nothing." Drew rubbed his head, "Look, I can't really talk to you. I promised... I promised Odd that I wouldn't let out any information that he didn't want out."

Cory was silent.

"I'm sorry." Drew said, "It's just not going to work right now."

"We can talk later." Cory agreed, "But I have some advice.

You? I found your name, your address, and some other info too, just from trails leading to your web store. Everything on the internet leaves a trail. Everything you do is recorded. Most people have their whole life story on it.

"But guess what? This Odd, I see nothing. I'm looking at my sources right now. I can get information about nearly anybody on the planet this way. I've just searched Odd, and all I get are a few random pieces of nonsense, none of them related to each other. So you say Odd made this product you're selling? That means only one thing."

"What?" Drew said. There was something weird about Cory's tone…

"You're being *set up*, Mr. Howell." Cory said bluntly, "The only person truly able to cover up their trail like that is either a hacker or a spy or both. I'm no expert, but this isn't good. You're in front, Mr. Howell. Say that thing has a virus in it, and it destroys everyone's computer that downloads it? Perhaps it'll steal their passwords and credit card numbers. Do you know this Odd? I mean, in person."

"No, but—"

"Exactly. First rule of an evil capitalist: make sure someone else takes the blame. If this thing is perfect, good for you, you get off great. If a single thing happens? It all comes down on your head, Mr. Howell. Odd's not going to be there. He won't exist. If he's smart enough to create what you have, then he's smart enough to never be found when we go looking."

"I… I think I need time to think." Drew said.

"Yes you do. I'll call later." Cory said, and then hung up before Drew even moved. Drew slumped in his chair. That Cory fellow made Odd sound, well, evil! But Drew trusted Odd completely.

Or at least he had used to.

CHAPTER 13

"Mom always said to be nice to the jerks. If you could be nice to a jerk, then you'd be happy. I don't see how getting hurt is supposed to make me happy."

–Arlen

Arlen's breathing was labored as he carried the letter. He thought he was doing the right thing, or at least it seemed like it. But the sun was rapidly rising, and Arlen had lost his chance to hunt in the night. He'd have to try doing it during twilight. That was not such a great idea, but Arlen had no choice. It didn't matter that the bugs would all be fleeing into hiding and he'd be flying under a hot sun, probably with nothing to bring home but an empty stomach. None of that mattered.

It was all because Arlen owed Lysander. Lysander had saved his life. It was just like Arlen's mom had said, so long ago, "You get help from somebody, you give it back, down to the last bug. The last speck of sand. Not many people do that, you know? You have to do that, it's the only thing people deserve from you. It's the only way you can be happy with yourself. Oh, sweetie, I know it sounds weird, and certainly most don't do it. But you have to. You must. You promise?"

"I promise." Arlen murmured to the memory. Then he shook his head and squeaked to find his position, pumping his wings hard to support the massive weight of paper he carried.

Don't think about mom now, he told himself. Not while he was concentrating on flying.

After all, he couldn't cry and fly at the same time. He didn't want to get his eye bandages wet. Arlen wondered if he could still cry.

But mom was the reason Arlen had to do all of this. Arlen had to repay Lysander for everything he had saved. And a life was worth a lot. If Lysander saved Arlen's life, that meant Arlen had to pay with his life. Or at least that's the way Arlen guessed it had to be. Nothing else made sense. He had even told this to Lysander.

Lysander agreed.

He let out a squeak, and almost tripped in the air when he realized with relief he was there. He could hear Haven right below him, and squeaked, memorizing the pattern of caves. Arlen dove for the one he knew was Lysander's, wings aching with the effort and the thought of being so close to done. But the sun was already peeking over the hills. Some bunnies were even out, jumping and diving back as Arlen came down. Arlen snickered. Bunnies sure were tense.

Arlen skidded on the ground, dropping the letter and landing none too gracefully. He went back up to get the dirtied envelope and, squeaking repeatedly, crept into the hole. He felt claustrophobic. The smell of old mold and unwashed rabbit wafted out. A cave was one thing, but this place wasn't even a scratch in the earth. How could bunnies stand it? The entire thing felt like it was going to collapse any second. Arlen would take good hard stone for his caves any day.

"Arlen?" Lysander's voice came in the darkness, "That you?"

"Yeah, *chirr*." Arlen said, squeaking. The odd, straight

lines stood out against the normal roughness of the cave. Those things Lysander had stolen with him sure were odd. Lysander said they did things, showed light and pictures. But even if Arlen could see, he was sure he wouldn't see that.

After all, Lysander was crazy.

"What do you want?" Lysander sounded annoyed, "I'm working."

Lysander was always working. Arlen shoved the letter forward, "This is for you, I think. Sorry, I shouldn't… I mean… You know the last letter? You said to put it on his door?"

"With the tape, yes." Lysander said, "Didn't it stick?"

"No, it did, eep!" Arlen said, "That weird clear thing… the tape, it stuck fine. But I barely got away before that human guy came out for those big rolls of paper on the doors—"

"Newspaper." Lysander said.

"Yeah, newspaper. *Chee.*" Arlen agreed instantly, no idea what Lysander meant. Lysander liked being agreed with. Arlen continued, "He took one look at it, and pulled it off, and then… he stuck that one on."

"A letter back?" Lysander said, his voice oddly flat, "I told him not to. I said not to send a letter back. Don't contact me, I said."

"Sorry." Arlen said.

"He *has* to listen!" Lysander said.

Arlen groaned inwardly. Here he was, trying to help, and now he had made Lysander angry. Big help he was.

"Doesn't he realize…" There was the sound of tearing paper. Arlen squeaked to see Lysander shredding the top open with his teeth. He held it up in front of the big, flat machine. The 'laptop', Lysander called it. He seemed to be reading. But how could he read deep in here? No light could get in here,

surely!

Unless that machine really did make light. No, impossible. Lysander was crazy. Arlen knew he had to be. After the things he had said, it was all too obvious Lysander had lost it.

"A *phone call*? He wants me to *call* him?" Lysander said out loud, his voice laced with acid, "A reporter? Why is he talking to reporters?"

"Maybe…" Arlen stopped himself. It wasn't his place.

"What?" Lysander asked.

"Maybe he um… well…" Arlen tried to find a nicer way to put it.

"Just say it, Arlen." Lysander said, "I don't have the time for this."

Arlen shrugged, his wings scraping the sides of the cave, "Maybe he disobeyed you."

The only sound in the cave was the resentful humming of machines.

"Who… who does he think he is?" Lysander's whole body coiled like a spring. Arlen took a few steps back. A bunny was supposed to cower under pressure. It was obvious Lysander was under pressure, but this wasn't cowering. He looked ready to bite something in half. This was Lysander's insanity. Arlen was growing convinced, day by day, that Lysander wasn't truly a bunny. He was one of… one of the machines. Like a car. Emotionless, no mercy and in total control at all times. Anything that got in his way was going to be run over. Arlen just hoped he wasn't going to be counted among the road kill. The thought made memories rise to his mind, and he felt sick to his stomach.

Arlen made a pathetic attempt at reason, "He's a human."

"So?" Lysander said.

"You're a bunny." Arlen said.

"Yeah, I got it. Bunny, bottom of the food web, huh? I eat grass, one step above the bottom. Everything wants to eat me." Lysander said, the sarcasm crackling like lightning, "And oh! A human! Humans are so powerful! No one ever, ever fights the humans. Do you know what a gun is, Arlen?"

Arlen didn't answer.

"I know you do. Every animal knows what a gun does. But did you know that even a human is killed by that gun? Guess what a gun does. Go on, guess."

Lysander continued without waiting for the answer, "It throws a little rock, it throws it so fast you can't even see. It's smaller than my eye, but it can take down a mountain lion. And if a human gets hit in the right spot, the heart or the brain or the lung or eye… that human is going to die. All we have to do," Lysander gestured to the screens behind him, "Is find that spot."

Arlen didn't move. Kill a human?

No. that was insane, even for Lysander. Was this how he was dealing with his problems? Planning to kill humans? That was impossible. A human couldn't be killed. Arlen had seen many dead things, but never a human. Humans never died. Humans were immortal, omnipotent.

"What?" Lysander said, "You look scared, Arlen. But it's not so different. We fear predators, but we don't blame them for what they do. It's how they live."

"But they eat what they kill." Arlen said, "You eat, *chirk*, plants."

"It doesn't matter what I eat!" Lysander said, "Don't you realize this has to be done?"

"Done?" Arlen was confused, "Why?"

"The humans... the humans aren't just in that little town. They are across the whole world, Arlen! This world has billions, *billions* of them. They control it. They have it all. No other animal can win. I'm just going to provide us with a chance."

Arlen asked, "How do —*eep!*— How do you know that? All those things?"

"Writing." Lysander stated simply, "I found my way into a place they call the library, and I figured it out. I know how to *read*, Arlen. That means every thought, everything a human has ever done... is mine to find out. And now I have a computer. The *internet*. I've been learning everything they know. They're teaching me how to defeat them."

"I don't understand." Arlen said.

Lysander suddenly screamed, "Well, I am *sick* of explaining!" Arlen took paces back, confronted by a bunny that now looked more like a wolf. Or a human. Lysander continued, "I explain and explain, all day long, but you animals, you animals don't understand. Humans have amassed more knowledge than you could learn in your entire life. Why do you animals have to be so *stupid?*"

"Lysander..." Arlen's voice tripped on his fear, "You're an animal too!"

Lysander stepped back, almost in surprise. Something had changed. But what? He looked smaller, somehow. Less dangerous.

Lysander's voice, still angry but quivering with something not unlike sadness, said softly, "Arlen, get out. Get out of here."

Arlen ran. Pure terror flooded through him, in his panic slamming into the walls of the cave and finally taking off just a second after he burst into the morning air. He had done it again. By trying to help, he had only caused more trouble. If

mother were here, she would comfort Arlen. Unfortunately, she was permanently absent in Arlen's life.

Arlen knew he should have been crying, but the tears just wouldn't come.

CHAPTER 14

"I don't get why people in charge think they're always right. It just means they mess up worse than normal people."

–Mirada

"Mirada!" Tysell's thick voice cut through the dark of the cave, "I knew I'd find you here!"

"Tysell?" Mirada turned, her heart jumping at the sound. Tysell sat at the mouth of the food stores, blocking what little light there was. Tysell's brownish-black fur seemed to fuzz out, hard to tell from the shadows.

"I don't know why you're worried," Mirada said quickly. "I'm just eating. Darshep said that we had extra—"

"Mirada!" Tysell groaned, and hopped up to her. She stuck her mouth right up to Mirada's face, her foul breath washing over her, "You're stealing for that freak. I've seen. But I don't tell, 'cuz we're friends. But you gotta stop. If Darshep finds out and I didn't tell him, we both get in trouble."

"We can't let him starve!" Mirada argued, trying to keep her voice low. Sound echoed all too well in caves.

"Hmph!" Tysell moved back. Mirada checked herself, sniffing for dirt. Sure enough, some had rubbed off of Tysell. She began to clean it off.

"Stop that!"

"I have to bring him food—"

"Not that!" Tysell grunted in disgust, "The cleaning. Half the day, you clean, clean, clean. Always keep yourself nice and shiny for those boy rabbits. And that little nose finds more food than anyone. You know me? Gotta work *all* day, and I can barely feed myself. No time to clean. My nose doesn't work like that. Can't get food like you all day."

Mirada frowned. With all the dirt on Tysell's nose, it was a wonder she could *breath*, let alone smell. She decided she probably shouldn't mention that.

"You still get a little from the food stores. Everyone does. No one starves."

"You know what? Fine. Whatever." Tysell sniffed, turning away, "You just keep on feeding that little freak of yours. Yeah, he's always shiny and clean too, isn't he? You'd fit perfect together. Yeah, Mirada, I know how you feel. You got a thing for that freako."

"I don't!" Mirada objected.

"Yeah! Yeah you do!" Tysell shouted.

Mirada stepped back, "What's this about, Tysell?"

"I've been your friend a long time. More than him! But remember last winter? We were on rations. Running outta food. And I was... *so* hungry. Figure, what's a few little roots? So I take some, but you see. And you tol' me, you said, 'Tysell, that's not fair. You want food, you find it yourself.'. So what's different with Lysander, huh?"

"I..." Mirada stopped. It was true; she had said those exact words.

"You can keep on stealing food for your friend. You got to, I know. I understand." Tysell said, her words throaty and harsh. Tysell's throat grated out another sentence, "And don't worry 'bout being friends, 'cuz guess what? I'm gonna tell Darshep. It's not you, it's just… like you said, it's not fair."

Tysell turned and began to hop down the caves. Mirada was after her in a shot, "Tysell! Wait! Wait up!"

Tysell was heading to the cave exit. Of course. Mirada tried to keep up, but she was too big, she bounced against the walls and slowed down, while Tysell was getting farther and farther away. She was going to tell, and then Mirada, and maybe even Lysander would be in big trouble. Mirada wasn't sure what Darshep could do, but she was sure she wouldn't like it.

Tysell was already outside the caves, shouting; "Darshep! Darshep, where are you?"

Mirada sprinted out into the blinding light, running headlong into the scrawny piece of dirt and fur that was Tysell. They tumbled down the hill together, rolling to a stop near the river.

Mirada, hurting all over, slowly rolled to her feet, "Oh, Tysell, I'm so sorry."

"Mirada." Tysell said, staring at her.

"Just listen! Lysander is… he's—"

"Mirada." Tysell said, and this time Mirada noticed Tysell wasn't looking at her. She was looking over her shoulder. Mirada turned to see what it was.

It was a nightmare. Dry red fur coated the long, thin creature. Three times their size, a long tail curling behind it like a snake.

A red fox. Second only to a wolf or coyote. It grinned down at them. Mirada's heart kicked into overdrive, slamming into her throat, but it wasn't helping. The fox was less than a foot away. They wouldn't get a step before it had them.

"Well!" The fox said, "Middle of the day too. Lucky." The

fox was toying with them. Mirada had heard that foxes liked to play with their food. Eat it alive, even. She was beginning to believe the rumors.

Mirada felt herself getting faint. Maybe she would have a heart attack even before the fox got her. Then she saw Darshep. He had come running, presumably because of Tysell's yelling. He was only five feet away, staring in horror.

"Yoo-hoo!" the fox called playfully, "Over here!"

Tysell shouted, "Darshep! Help!"

Darshep stepped forward, as if to help, but stopped. Then he ran for Haven, the safety of the caves. Mirada felt betrayed, but really, what could Darshep do? He was a bunny. He may have acted tough, but he was just a bunny.

"Oh, too bad. Three could have been even better. Alright, little bunny buddies." The fox snarled, "Say goodbye so I can get on with my meal. You have until I start drooling."

Mirada and Tysell looked at each other, but were silent. What was there to say? But Mirada noticed something in Tysell's eyes. The meaning, even without it being said out loud, was obvious. *Sorry.*

Me too. Mirada tried to say back. Tysell managed a tiny grin.

"That's it? Wow." the fox said.

It coiled, ready to spring.

"STOP!"

The fox, Mirada, and Tysell turned to see the voice. Something, a blinding white flash, was streaking down the hill. It tripped, rolling and running into Mirada and Tysell. A moment later, the thing scrambled to its feet.

"Lysander?" Mirada gasped. What was he doing here? He was crazy!

He was insane.

"Back off, dog!" Lysander hissed, stalking towards the fox. The fox actually drew back a pace, confused.

It sneered, "I am no *dog*, you rodent. I bow to no human."

"I think you do." Lysander said, moving right up to the fox's nose and staring it right in both eyes. Mirada gasped aloud. Wasn't he afraid?

"You're certainly an odd little bunny. But wrong." The fox grinned, "If a human were here, he'd be afraid of *me*."

"Liar." Lysander said, flecks of spit flying from his mouth, "Maybe a wolf could scare a human, but you're not even close. If you heard even one human, heard a single human word, you would stick that big fluff pile between your legs and head for the hills."

"Prove it, fluffy." The fox hissed.

Lysander, grinning widely, took a step back. He sat back on his hind legs, and swung one arm forward to point at the fox. Lysander's mouth opened, oddly wider, and from it came deep, biting sounds. Sounds that, though Mirada couldn't tell why, struck her heart and made it flutter, the cold darkness of unconsciousness threatening to grab her once more.

The fox's eyes went wide, his pupils shrinking even as he seemed to shrink. He jumped backwards, giving a great yelp, and then, scrambling to find purchase on the slope, tail between his legs.

He ran.

The world was silent except for rushing water. Mirada managed to get ahold of herself, and gulping, asked, "What was *that*? Why did… how did you scare off…"

"Mirada!" Tysell whispered. Mirada turned to see Tysell. She was shaking convulsively, her chest heaving and her eyes

wide, fixed on Lysander. He just stood there, stock-still and angry.

"What?" Mirada asked.

"Those words… those words Lysander said." Tysell's voice was filled with an unfathomable terror, "Those were *human* words."

CHAPTER 15

"We assume lots of things. We assume our food is edible, that our phone isn't going to electrocute us. The only problem is that all that assuming makes lies pretty easy."

–Cory Yalk

Drew ducked into the back room, checking over his shoulder anxiously. The angry man from the other day was there, arched over a box of discount country music CDs. Drew decided that when the man came to find out what had happened to his computer, he wouldn't be the one to tell him.

The computer was fixed, thankfully. Drew had to go on multiple internet sites, and finally found one on an online garage sale. An identical computer. He had swapped out almost every part except the hard drive. It seemed to work now. But even so, Drew couldn't bring himself to talk to the man. If anything went wrong, such as the man realizing he actually had to pay for repairs, that would mean yelling. Drew couldn't take that again.

He heard the phone in the back room, and practically ran for it. No one else was there, and he ripped the phone out of the socket before another employee picked it up somewhere else in the store. It was an excuse, and Drew decided to take it.

"Hello, *Bunny Computers.* How may I help you?"

"It's me. Odd."

Drew fumbled with the handset, almost dropping it in shock. He looked around the back room, making sure no one was watching. Holding the handset tightly, he bolted for his office, running in and slamming the door behind him. Slumping in his seat, he breathed in deeply the smell of ink toner and the air freshener he had gotten for his birthday. Jess had given him the air freshener.

"You there?" Drew finally asked.

"Yeah, right here." Odd replied. The voice was oddly high-pitched, and with the strangest accent, like Odd was whistling whenever he talked. It was almost robotic.

"So you decided we could talk."

"Yes…" Odd paused, and Drew got the feeling something was wrong. Odd continued, "Look, not best day ever for me. I had fight with friends, and your letter, and now had to steal phone to call you."

"Don't you… don't you have a phone? Or use a pay phone!" Drew said. It was hard to understand Odd through the accent. His letters were written that way too, Drew realized.

"I am not having phone. I am, see, you see…" Odd seemed to be searching for the right word, "Busted."

"Busted?" Drew asked, raising an eyebrow.

"Yeah. Busted." Odd said.

"I'm not sure I understand you."

"Busted! It is the expression! The English thingy!"

Drew realized something, "You mean broke?"

Odd sighed, "Yah."

"But… Drew tapped his computer, which woke up showing information screens, "That website has earned like, a quarter million dollars so far, and it's only been a few months!"

"It is your company. I do not get money."

Drew could have hit himself, "Oh, right. Sorry."

"Why did you want to talk to me?" Odd asked.

Drew leaned back in his chair, trying to choose his words carefully, "Well… I'm just anxious, worried a little."

"Why?"

"Well, it's just… there was this reporter, and he asked a lot of questions. He even said you might be a hacker—"

"I am not hacker."

"Right. But what am I supposed to do if they keep asking me questions? What do I tell them? I have to say something!"

Odd was silent on the other end of the line. Drew waited, tapping his computer screen impatiently. Ripples bubbled across the screen. It probably wasn't the wisest thing to do, that could break the entire screen, but Drew couldn't stop himself. He was too nervous, which brought out his twitchiness. He had developed that nervous twitch working with animals, especially the ones sick with rabies. It was good to have quick reflexes in those situations.

Odd said, "It is your company. All yours. Tell them I am nice person. I am shy. I do not want company of my own. But I like the world to use my programs. So I give to you, and you sell."

Drew nodded, "And how can I be sure it doesn't have viruses or anything in the programs?"

"You cannot know. I know, and I say there is none. You trust me, yah?"

"Yah— I mean, okay." Drew shook his head tiredly, "I suppose you won't be calling me back?"

Odd seemed to think about it a moment, "How much you say you earn from website?"

"Fifty thousand, give or take." Drew said, "So far. I mean,

it's only been a few months..." Even his own voice sounded skeptical, but it was true.

"Is that payment good for stolen computer?"

Drew was confused, "Well, yes, of course." How foreign was Odd if he didn't know what fifty thousand dollars was worth?

Odd said, "Then I owe you nothing. Could I ask favor?"

"Why not?" Drew said, "You've done me some."

"Could you buy phone, give to me? Then we talk if have to."

"Well, sure."

"I will pay back for phone too." Odd said, "In two days, I send next letter. Very important. Very big letter."

"Okay."

"I call you. No call me. Leave phone you buy on car roof." Odd said. Drew opened his mouth to reply, but the phone clicked. Odd had hung up.

If Drew had any hope of guessing who Odd was before, he sure didn't now.

Odd moved fast. He called at one in the morning, from the phone Drew had put on his car roof at eight the night before. Drew was shocked out of his sleep by the buzz of the phone next to his ear. He shot up in bed, grabbing it and reading the caller-ID. The number he had already put in his contacts as 'Odd'. He blearily got out of bed, Jess sitting up in bed behind him.

She mumbled, "Whuzzat?"

"Just some work things, dear." Drew said, not wanting to mention Odd, "Go to bed, I'll only take a minute." He walked out of the room, flipping the phone open. Instinctively, he kept his footsteps light, looking at the ground. This part was near the kitchen, though, and was mostly spotless.

"Hello?" He asked as he entered the living room and fell onto the couch. It wasn't very comfortable, too hard, designed to retain a perfect stylish plumpness, even if a train hit it. The room was built that way, the glass chandelier made of hardened plexiglass, the piano's wheels welded so they wouldn't roll. Jess had designed it.

Finally, sound came from the phone, "It is finished. Finished my project. Go up to your computer. I have e-mailed you the files."

"Is that you, Odd?" Drew asked.

"Yes! Yes, why wouldn't it be me?"

Drew didn't say anything. It was Odd's voice, almost, but it was like the accent was faded, gone a little bit. The words were more fluent. It was like the Odd he had heard before, but off in such a way that disturbed him more than he would like to admit.

"Have you gone to the computer?" Odd asked.

"Just a second." Drew got up, groaning a little, and moved to his office. Inside, piles of invoices for pet supplies languished in the corner, while a new, shiny computer, a prototype from the store, gleamed on the desk. All the invoices at the computer store were electronic. Drew turned it on, eyes glazing over as it booted up. He sat down, logged in, and opened the e-mail. Clicking on the new letter, he tapped the attachments. It was a picture. No, it was a blueprint. Drew's eyes sharpened, trying to make out what he was seeing.

Drew asked, "What is it?"

"It is our new product. We sell software, yes? Now we sale

hardware."

"Hardware?" Drew asked, and then began to make sense of it. He was looking at some kind of computer, zoomed in a hundred times its size. But these little lines couldn't be wires, they were crossed all over, jumbled up in meaningless patterns. Not like the straight lines and turns of real computers.

"Are you sure about this?" Drew said.

"You have to trust me." Odd said, sending a shiver up Drew's spine.

Drew said, "I've been meaning to talk to you about that. You know the guy who called me? See, I was meaning to say—"

"We must have a factory." Odd said over him, "I have a building company for you to call. Instructions are in the e-mail."

"Right." Drew said, feeling something was off about Odd's voice, "But—"

"I cannot have you disobeying orders."

Drew opened his mouth, but no words came out. Odd's voice was deadly serious, "We can make lots of money, Drew, but you must do what I say, yes? You must follow orders. I earned you lots of money so far, but this isn't going to cut it. We need to use that money, grow bigger. We need more, Drew, and then you'll get everything, everything you want. No more worries, enough money to last you the rest of your life. Wouldn't that be nice?"

"Yes—"

"Then follow the instructions, and *no more questions*."

Odd hung up.

Drew sat back in his chair, staring at the light of his computer, eyes glazed and unseeing. He had really done it now, hadn't he? He was in deep now, and Odd was driving. Odd

scared him. By the end of that call, the accent was all but gone. How had he switched like that? He had a huge accent that morning. It was like in a few calls, he had gotten rid of it completely, even adopting the heavy, slurred Utah accent that Drew had carried his whole life.

Drew stood up. He needed to talk to somebody. He moved to the door, heading for his bedroom and Jess. Then he stopped. She wouldn't believe him about the accent, she hadn't believe him about seeing Glossy on the road. She was asleep, too, something Drew wouldn't be able to do.

Drew turned back, staring at the computer. The e-mail sat open, beckoning to him. He sat down, and read. He didn't want to read, but he did. Because in his mind, Odd's powerful, strange voice echoed.

Follow the instructions.

CHAPTER 16

"Fainting is a wonderful thing. It's your body's way of saying 'Hey, is life being tough? Time for a break!'"

–Zach Erikson

Of course, Mirada fainted. It was only natural. Sure, she could handle almost everything, but this was different. Even weird things, things that had been causing near-panic to the other bunnies, hadn't worried her so much. She could stand the wire filled with lightning heading up to Lysander's hole, and she could handle the odd 'machines' that made light and weird noise.

She didn't need to understand why Lysander acted the way he did. He was so smart, there had to be a good reason. Of course, the way Lysander stood up to that fox wasn't insane or scary, that was heroic!

But *human speech.*

That was different. That was... Mirada wanted to say foul, but that wasn't quite right. Not for Lysander, he couldn't do anything like that. No, there was some other explanation. Maybe those humans had done something to him.

That was it. You couldn't control what the humans did, and so they did something to Lysander! Mirada knew about that, she had once been held captive by them. Her and her

parents, plus six siblings. They had all been in one big cage together, in a little wooden shack somewhere. She remembered the cold wire of the cage, her claws catching on the holes. It was so small, too, the water stagnant in a dish that she often panicked and stepped in, the food pellets dry and with more of a catastrophic smashing of flavors than any recognizable plant taste. And so cramped. Cramped that you felt you could barely breath, that one day your heart would pop right out of your mouth, trying to escape the confines of metal.

At least she had escaped. When a human had gotten her out, and she had panicked. The human had dropped her, and she ran for her life. She had been outside the wooden shack, with the woods nearby and no fence in her way. Of course, she had left her parents and everyone else behind, but at least she had gotten free.

Off into the wild unknown. Go to the wild. That's what her mother had always said to her. Sure, they got fed in the cage, mom had said, but it was nothing compared to freedom. That's what she'd been told. Mirada's mom had been captured as a tiny bunny, and had raised her family in the cage. Good girl that she was, Mirada trusted her mother's words.

Never before had that been so wrong.

Mirada's heart ached for her family, wanting to free them more than anything. She couldn't, of course. She couldn't try to beat the humans that had them captive, for whatever horrible reason. Why had they done it? What was the use of holding animals in cages? Not for eating, not for anything. Just for cruelty. Their personal, sick enjoyment.

Mirada lay on the ground, shivering against the coming night that she had woken up to. Had she been out all day? Her stomach told her yes. She was lucky no other predators had

come along.

Mirada began to hop slowly up the hill, thinking. So, maybe Lysander knew human speech. No, of course not. Maybe he knew a few words. That was all. Maybe six or seven, that was it. And this explained his behavior, of course! He acted strangely because the humans had done something to him. That was it. Mirada could only imagine what horrible things Lysander must have gone through.

When she got up to Lysander's hole, she paused. A bunny, or some other animal, guarded the entrance. Not Lysander, it had dark fur. And almost too small for a bunny. Very small.

"Who's that?" It asked softly, it's voice shivery on the air, "*Chirk!* Mirada?"

"Arlen? Arlen of Darkdoor cave?" Mirada asked, "What are you doing here?"

"Just go away." Arlen said, "You can't see Lysander right now, *chee.* He's busy." Arlen's voice quivered, like he was extremely tired. But weren't bats awake at night?

"Are you okay, Arlen?" Mirada asked kindly. She knew Arlen because of Lysander. He came every morning, and sometimes night, to get orders and deliver things for Lysander. Apparently, Lysander had saved him just like he had saved her.

Arlen sighed, "No, not really. I... I've not had any sleep since yesterday evening. I was up all night, doing things for Lysander, then I wanted to catch some bugs and get some sleep this morning, and I did after me and Lysander had a fight. Or I started to, *chir.*" Arlen was now a little visible, Mirada's eyes adjusting to the darkness. In the cave a light glowed.

Arlen continued, "Then, *cheep*, he called me back when I was just about to get to sleep, and we've been working since —*chee*— since then. And now I'm guarding."

But Arlen suddenly moved forward, getting close to Mirada, "But you really don't want to see him, he's... he's gone crazy. Today he even used... used what sounded like—"

"Human speech." Mirada finished.

"Yeah." Arlen finished, "*Chirk!*"

"Look, he's not crazy!" Mirada burst out.

"What?"

"All you animals are always like, blah blah, Lysander's crazy, he's going to do something horrible... well, how do you think *he* feels, all the time? Nobody cares about him, they'd let him *starve* if I didn't... if I didn't..." Mirada trailed off, feeling horrible. She couldn't meet Arlen's eyes. Of course, that probably didn't matter in Arlen's case.

Arlen made a few chirps, "Mirada, he *is* crazy, there's no other way about it."

"Then why'd he save me just now? He saved my life! He saw I was in danger and he was there, just like he was there for you."

"I can't answer that." Arlen said, "He's kind when a life is in danger. When that happens he's... incredible. Any other time he's heartless. Sorry." Arlen shook his head, like he was ashamed of what he said. "I don't know why he saved me, but I... I wish he hadn't."

"Oh... be quiet." Mirada sniffled, turning away.

Arlen was suddenly by her, "I understand how you feel. He's different, above it all for good or bad. And you like that. So many people look down when he looks up. That's why you like him. Because he's better."

"He's wonderful." Mirada said, and then shivered.

"Yeah, okay." Arlen sighed, "Look, Mirada, I don't... I can never understand him. You know him better than anyone."

"I hardly know him!"

"You *hardly* know him. Anybody else has *no* idea at all." Arlen said, "Look, I… a lot of animals have been asking me, bats and rabbits and even others, about him, and… I don't want to tell them bad things. That's all I have right now, though. He saved you and Tysell, and he saved me." Arlen paused, "And if I knew why, well…"

"You could have something good to say." Mirada grinned, "Arlen, that's great!"

"I do what I can." Arlen said, his voice shaking, "So, Lysander ordered me to not let anyone in, but maybe you could… slip in without me seeing?"

"How would I… oh." Mirada remembered the bandage over Arlen's eyes, "I get it."

"He's in a bad mood. Good luck. *Chirk!*" Arlen's squeaks were starting to hurt Mirada's ears, and she nearly asked him to stop. That was the only way he could see, though, so she didn't say anything.

"Thanks Arlen." Mirada said, moving softly past him to the cave entrance. She began to move quicker, but stopped, and looked back.

Arlen stood there, looking up, straight at the moon, smiling quietly. How could he see it? Mirada felt a sick, twisted feeling in her chest. He really had been awake until yesterday evening, hadn't he? Working for Lysander the entire time. And Lysander hadn't given him a single break, Arlen hadn't even eaten… But yet Arlen had done it all. He had done it all and even wanted to spread good things about Lysander, though he himself said Lysander was crazy. No animal was like that, especially a bat. Not even Lysander. The bat with no eyes, few family, and not even any friends. Of course, he wanted to help, so didn't that make it okay?

So why did Mirada feel so guilty?

 STEVEN OLSEN - 102

CHAPTER 17

"There's two types of people. There's the people that see the flaws in others, and see they're perfect, and there's those that see others as perfect, and they're flawed. So which one is right?"

–Mirada

Mirada, true to form, did a quick check-up before interrupting Lysander. She cleaned her fur, checked her claws, blinked and made herself cry to wash out her eyes, licked her teeth, and cleaned again. Finally, she hopped a few steps forward. Lysander stood in the cave, lit by the glow of that huge rectangle. His paws rested on a tiny device, a new one.

"Lysander, are you okay?" Mirada said. Lysander only scowled deeper at the device.

Mirada tried again, "Lysander?"

He looked up, "How'd you get in? Arlen didn't desert his post, did he?"

"Well, no." Mirada said, frowning at Lysander's angry tone.

"Good." Lysander said, taking his paw off the device and smacking it into a corner, "Because I'm done with people questioning my orders. I haven't had any food all day."

"I'm sorry." Mirada said, "I fainted, after, you know…"

Lysander looked away, "Whatever. Just don't forget tomorrow. I'm too busy to get it myself, you know. If I stop

now…" He paused, "You understand, right? You know I need support, that I'm the only one who can do this."

"Yes, of course!" Mirada said. After a second, she asked, "Do what?"

"The humans!" Lysander gestured at the glowing thing, like that made it obvious, and swept a paw behind him at the blinking lights, "The machines!"

Mirada looked down, "Lysander… can I ask you something?"

"Make it quick. I'm behind schedule."

"Why did you save us? From the fox, I mean."

"I know what you mean." Lysander turned, looking away from her at a dark corner of the cave, "Darshep was off screaming about the fox, and I heard, so I came down and did what I could. Great load of help that did me."

"I know." Mirada said, shifting her feet. She was so nervous, shaking like a leaf, "But why?"

"I–" Lysander's voice caught, "None of your business."

Mirada stepped forward, "It's your parents, isn't it?"

Lysander's angry shivers stopped. It was like somebody had dumped him in the winter river and froze him solid how he stood.

Mirada forced herself to go on, "It's just… you're a lot like Arlen. He lost his parents too, you know. Everyone knows. He's actually a little famous because of it. They got… a car got them, blinded them with its lights. You know how it is, your mind goes blank, and you can't move… and the light hurts so much—" Mirada shook her head, "But they're gone, now, and Arlen was left all alone. It was so unlikely, you know. Cars almost never hit flying things, and it got both of them. Apparently the light was so bright they just fell out of the sky,

and went under the tires… Now Arlen doesn't have anybody. Except for his colony, of course. Same for me.

"But you can't forget, huh? Instinct is good, but parents… they tell you everything. My dad, I remember, he took one look at my nose, and he said, 'You're a smeller, Mirada! I nose it!' Get it? Nose?" Mirada giggled and hiccupped, feeling tears at the corners of her eyes, "He was always making jokes like that, probably still is, wherever he is now."

Lysander turned towards her, ignoring the machines, "What was your mom like?"

"Mom?" Mirada smiled, feeling her nervous quivers fade even as the tears came up. Tears that were sad from loss, but happy from remembering, "Mom didn't take any slack from me. She always expected us to be survivors, able to stroll right out into the wild where she came from and live there as easily as if the humans still brought us food. She expected a lot, actually. But she wasn't all mean! She loved us, we always knew that. She just was so hard because she didn't want to see anything happen to us, you know?"

"Yeah." Lysander said softly.

"What about yours?" Mirada asked, "What were your parents like?"

"I… I don't remember." Lysander choked out, his voice brimming with emotion Mirada almost never saw. Maybe the shock was finally getting to him. The shock of the fox and everyone's hateful whispers and homesickness. Lysander said, "Ever since… my accident. I remember them, I know they were in the store with me, but it's just so fuzzy… I can't…"

"But you know." Mirada said, "That they loved you, I mean."

Lysander's chest heaved in and out, his heart pattering so

hard Mirada could see the vibrations, "I think... I think... yes. Yes."

"See? I think that's the reason we have parents. So someone cares. And then they leave. But that's the way it is." Mirada said, "Parents go away. Most animals die, and I'm actually lucky. Mine might still be alive, somewhere. And Arlen, both his parents and just one car... You said cars were used by humans, a machine? That means we all lost them to humans, didn't we? You, me, and Arlen. Most animals have at least one parent, but us, the humans took them all."

"They did." Lysander said, "The humans!" A light glinted in his eyes, "They made it so I can't remember, didn't they? And they aren't even predators. Why do they do it, Mirada? Why?"

"I don't know." Mirada said, "You can't ask why, Lysander. It's... It's the humans! No one asks why about a human."

"Of course they don't. Just like they never asked about the cars, or the power lines, or the lights in the buildings. They never asked what those were." Lysander said, "And look where that's got us. Stuck in a hole on a cliff, praying a fox doesn't show up and eat us all."

"But at least we're alive." Mirada said.

"At least we're alive." Lysander said, his voice sad, "That's all that matters, isn't it? At least to a bunny."

"What else is there?"

"You have no idea." Lysander said, turning away again. Mirada, not wanting to lose the chance she had worked so hard for, struggled to find courage. Then she inched closer to Lysander.

Mirada began, "All I ever knew was staying alive. Find food, eat it, stay hidden, stay alive." She paused, "But you know more somehow. Is that why you helped us?"

"I don't know why." Lysander said, "I can't remember a thing… If I ever try, I get this huge headache… and all I can remember is that I was in the pet store, and there were my parents, I think… and other little bunnies like me. And they all began to disappear. Each day, more were gone. All I know is that… when I saw Arlen, and when I heard Darshep yelling about you… I just had to. I couldn't stop, and I knew I'd probably end up dying myself, but I just had to."

Lysander sucked in a breath, breathing so hard it was like he was attempting to inhale water. After a second, he said, "I just… Arlen sometimes talks about his mom, how she always talked about being nice. It's like that's all she talked about. Whenever he talks about that, it makes me think of… of my mom, for some reason, and I think… I think she was like that, and every time I see somebody in trouble, like Arlen or you, it makes me think of her. It makes me think about when… when they took her…"

Lysander shook his head, tears flecking off his face, "I just can't let that happen a second time."

"If only that power line hadn't hit you." Mirada said, "Then you probably *could* remember. You could remember the good times with your mom."

"Yeah." Lysander said. He took a deep breath, "All I got from that thing was headaches and talking like a stupid… I can't say it. Even the name hurts now. But I feel better. I guess it was maybe because of Arlen. I helped you because he said something today, reminded me."

"Reminded you?" Mirada asked.

"Or something." Lysander shook his head, "He said something that wasn't very nice. Well, it was just a fact but it was something I didn't want to hear. He didn't mean it that way, but it's how it made me feel. When he said that, it… it hurt, a lot. It was like I was sleeping and somebody screamed in my ear so hard it hurt. It woke me up, though. I feel… so…"

Lysander shook his head, "I feel angry at humans, and scared of that fox, and confused and sad and happy that I'm alive, and… I just want it to *stop*." He spat out the last word, "I don't want to deal with it anymore. I want to just go back to the plan, and not think about it anymore."

He sat for a second, and Mirada did too, wondering what was going on. Lysander sounded so hurt, his voice spilling over with so many emotions that the words couldn't contain them all. It was like they had all been held in, contained somewhere, and today they came rushing out.

That had to be why he had helped her, he couldn't control himself. He saw her problem and his emotions took control. That's why he had been so incredibly stupid and brave, he wasn't thinking straight. Mirada could only be grateful that had happened.

She looked across at him, smiling, and then frowned. Something was wrong. Lysander's eyes were misted over, staring at something far away. The same expression as before, the one Mirada wasn't too fond of. He was frowning, and like a dark fog, the words slid from his mouth.

Lysander said, "It's *their* fault. The humans did this to me, you know. All of this to everyone."

Lysander sat up, eyes focusing, "I have to work." He went to the machine, the glowing rectangle, and began to type. Mirada turned, mouth open and totally put off. She hopped forward, trying to think of something, *anything*, to say.

Then she stopped. She had realized that she wasn't doing what she needed to. The bunny in front of her wasn't Lysander.

Lysander was the bunny she cared about, who dove in to save others, who cared about parents and other's stories. But this wasn't that Lysander. This was someone different. A bunny that was obsessed with machines and humans and other things.

A bunny that controlled, that had no mercy where Lysander would step in to lend a helping hand.

Was that it? It had to be. The thing in front of her hunched over the buttons, pounding away at rapid speed and not giving a thought to her. She no longer existed in that *thing's* knowledge. That wasn't Lysander. Lysander wasn't crazy, this is what it was! This was the problem! This is what had yelled at her when she came in, what commanded Arlen to guard the door.

Now Mirada knew. What made it all the worse is that she had no idea how to fix it.

CHAPTER 18

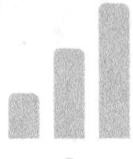

*"Why is it that sometimes bad things happen
to me when all I'm trying to do is help?"*

–Arlen

"Hey! Arlen!" A group of bats greeted the tired Arlen as he
circled down towards the caves that night. It was a rather cold
night, the first noticeable one all summer. Arlen wondered at
the weather, surely winter couldn't be that close already. Arlen
squeaked, figuring out who the bats were. He recognized his
brother, "Oh, hey Fallon. What's going on?"

"You are." Fallon said, flapping alongside Arlen, "Where
were you tonight? We all went hunting without you. Did you
get any food at all?"

"Yeah." Arlen said, "I caught some bugs after Lysander
said I could go."

"That's all you think about anymore." One of Fallon's
backup, Tolluri, said, "That Lysander bunny."

Arlen ignored him, getting in the caves and finding a free
spot to latch his claws into. He wrapped his wings around himself, tired from everything. He could finally get some sleep. But
Fallon and Tolluri landed next to him, and several other bats
were starting to gather around.

"Tolluri's right, Arlen." Fallon said, "You're spending

more time doing what that Lysander says than… than looking for food!"

"I'm sorry.' Arlen said, "I just… I owe him."

"You don't… Arlen, look." Fallon came closer to Arlen, rubbing up against him, "You don't owe that Lysander a thing. Yeah, I know what mom always said. Be nice to everyone, even your enemies. You are pretty nice, lots more than me. But with the way he acts, the way he uses you… you're almost better off dead. So you've repaid him."

"That's not what mom would say."

"Mom is dead." Fallon said, causing Arlen to flinch, "Sometimes I think you don't realize that."

"I know, Fallon." Arlen said, "But I've got to help him. I don't think he could survive in the wild, you know?"

"Then you're saving his life, huh? Every day you save his sorry life, you and that other bunny that takes him food. I've been watching." Fallon said. Tolluri nodded in agreement.

"You were watching?"

"I'm worried about you." Fallon drew closer, squeaking right in Arlen's ear, "I'm not going to let anything happen to you, even if you don't care about yourself. You need to look out for you, Arlen. I've seen how you look lately. You fly crooked. You're sleepy all the time. If something happens to you, how are you supposed to help this loser anyway?"

"I don't know, Fallon. I don't know what to do. I can't just stop helping him! Mom wouldn't and I won't. Just because you forget kindness doesn't mean I have to. I don't want to be… *you*. That was mean. Sorry."

Fallon waved to his friends, muttering something. They took off, going to roost in dark corners of the cave. Fallon said, "I know you can't. If there's something nice you can do, you do it, no matter the consequences. If I was thirsty you would kill yourself to get me a drink of water."

"That's ridiculous!"

Fallon shook his head, "You would. You don't think so, but I know you would. I'm not going to let you be under that bunny's paw forever, Arlen. I don't care what I have to do. I know what you think about me. As nice as you are, you don't like how I lead our clan.

"Well, sometimes I have to do things that aren't so nice. But it's for good. You want to do nice things, and you don't care about what the consequences are. I'm going to make things better, even if that means I have to do one or two not so great things to get that done. You follow?"

"The ends justify the means." Arlen said, "You've told me before." He looked away, hating what he had just said. It was true, but it wasn't nice to say out loud.

Since Fallon had taken over, that had been practically the motto. It had used to be that bats did what they wanted, just formed a mob group and tried to catch as many bugs as they could eat every night. Fallon had always complained about that. Arlen had assumed he was complaining because he often got the short end of the stick. He wasn't quite quick enough to get as much food as others, and sometimes they would swoop in front of him and take the bugs he was going to eat, just to mock him. He got enough food, of course, but occasionally was still a little hungry.

Then, when Fallon grew up, it changed. He got friends of his together, and they would recruit others. They would compare notes, go out on bug hunts together. Watch for predators together. It worked so well that everyone wanted to be involved in Fallon's group. Eventually, he rose to so much power that he

could say whatever he wanted, and it was done.

Arlen wasn't complaining. At least, he wasn't trying to. It was true that the clan rarely went hungry anymore, with all bug locations reported to Fallon and all the bats hunting together. Even better, there was a sense of unity in the cave, certain rules in place so that all the bats had safety and they were required to act a certain way to each other. There was no fighting or yelling allowed. Talking and squeaking during sleeping hours was also kept to a minimum, which was nice.

The only problem was that with so much power, Fallon was starting to realize the ways he could use it. It was common knowledge that breaking a rule meant having a not-so-friendly talk with Fallon and pals. Those who broke rules multiple times might get thrown around or beaten up on Fallon's orders. Trying to usurp Fallon's power or breaking a rule repeatedly could even result in eviction. Being thrown from the cave into the wild, all alone. A death sentence would have been a more precise term.

Fallon said, "I'd rather have a good end, and a bad past, then good now and bad in the end. The past is behind me, but I live in the present. So yeah, like you said. If that bunny doesn't change something soon, if he doesn't stop talking about humans and cars, and if he keeps using you… I'm going to fix that."

"No, Fallon." Arlen said, "You wouldn't."

"Don't lie to yourself, Arlen." Fallon said, "You know what I'd do."

"I have to warn him, at least."

"I don't think so. If you warn him, he might change, but that'll be to avoid me. It won't be because he really wants to change. It'll all be a lie, and I'm not standing for that. You warn him and you'll be in just as much trouble."

"I won't let you near him." Arlen said, "Fallon, I won't let you! You're my brother, but this is crazy! I've seen... what you do." Arlen cringed.

"I hate it too." Fallon said, bowing his head, "I do it because I have to, Arlen. Someone around here has to bring justice. Mom even said that people will pay for their evil deeds."

"She didn't mean that." Arlen said, "She didn't mean that you're the one who makes them pay."

Fallon broke off, flapping to a distant part of the cave, "Well, I do."

CHAPTER 19

"He's building that empire on a mob, people. He's turning you into a mob, and he's going to ride on your backs, using you all as his throne. You poor, stupid people."

–Cory Yalk

The factory was built in two months, and a month later Drew was a millionaire.

Well, almost a millionaire. Technically all the money he had was from pre-orders, people purchasing the thing before it was even made, and waiting until the factory finally popped it out. Some of that money would be used in making the product; some of it would go to taxes. But the orders were piling up fast, only speeding up and never slowing down. Drew had to switch to double shifts at the factory and then round-the-clock production, but even that wasn't enough. Every time he sent out a computer he'd receive orders for three more. He had to hire people from around the state and then start shipping them in from other parts of the country. The construction companies that he had hired for the factory were assigned to make apartment complexes to hold the employees until there was time to build houses. Drew began phone calls to build three more factories.

Some around town were saying it was impossible. No one could make that much money, no matter what they were

selling. Perhaps, they whispered, Drew had been doing some back deals, illegal gambling. Drew tried to ignore them, which wasn't hard. He had other things to do, many more things.

He could barely keep up with Odd's orders. Letters would arrive almost every day, mostly on Drew's porch. Odd still didn't like talking on the telephone, and so kept most of his communication to letters or, if he was in a hurry, e-mail. Drew had stayed up one night, sure he would catch Odd as he snuck up to the doorstep. He had watched all night, half asleep. Then the letter had dropped from the sky. He had run outside in a flash, but was greeted by nothing but crickets and the dry summer night. Drew reminded himself sourly that he was going to have to be a lot smarter than that if he wanted to outsmart his new friend.

So Drew had no choice but to follow Odd's commands. Odd was always demanding speed, which is what had driven Drew to hire multiple construction companies to work together on a single factory, an experience he hadn't liked too much. But it was working. The thing, the product that Drew himself didn't fully understand, was selling by truckloads. It was only available on Drew's website, delivered by mail, and only payable by credit card. It defied all logic, but as Drew was quickly finding, Odd wasn't always very logical.

Not always logical, but always right.

It had all gone fine until everyone noticed they were buying it. It actually took a while for people to realize how popular the thing was becoming. When they did, reporters began to call.

On Odd's orders, Drew began to take interviews. He talked to the news and the newspapers, the bloggers and really anyone else who was going to spread the word. It was, after all,

free advertising. The only problem was that the questions, usually normal, harmless, sometimes caused him to give the wrong answers. The first mistake had been with a TV reporter, one that had flown down to interview him and a few other people.

She had been pretty, at least from far away, but as Drew got closer her face seemed unusual, exaggerated for the camera but odd looking at close range. He decided to ignore the makeup, though. He invited her into his new office above the factory production floor, and they both sat. Drew hadn't had time to move anything into the office besides bare essentials. He barely had time to do anything but bare essentials anymore.

"So," The young reporter asked Drew, crossing her legs, "Tell me about yourself. Do you have a lot of programming experience?" She looked around the office, mouth smiling but eyes narrowed in distaste.

Drew said, "Well, no. None, actually."

The reporter cocked her head, "Interesting. One might assume that to have made the things you sell, you'd have to have a lot of programming knowledge."

"Oh, I didn't make it." Drew said, and grimaced as he noticed what he had just said. The reporter leaned forward, her tight dress creasing and her fake eyelashes popping an inch, "Then who did?"

Drew resigned himself, and smiling, said, "Well, he calls himself Odd."

"Odd? That's an, um, *odd* name." The reporter said awkwardly, "So you have a business agreement with Odd? He's the inventor, and you're the businessman?"

"No. I mean yes. That is, the present was kind of a gift. I mean, he gave it to me." Drew said, flubbing up, "But let's talk about something else."

"But this is interesting!" The reporter waved her hands to demonstrate the fact, "How long have you known this fellow?"

"Um, some months… maybe since the start of summer."

"That's an awful short time for him to like you so much. What does he get out of this whole thing?"

"He hasn't asked for anything."

The reporter gaped, "Really…?" Her voice dripped with interest, everything she said was pronounced so clearly and loudly that Drew wondered what he was going to sound like in comparison.

"Really." Drew smiled weakly, "Once he asks, I'll be happy to repay him in whatever way I can. But he hasn't asked for a thing, not in one of his letters."

"Letters? As in, the mail? Don't you ever talk to him?"

"Once or twice. But usually he just sends letters… look, he's really a very private, very um… I'd rather not talk about this anymore."

The reporter smiled, "Of course, we should wait until later, when we can get an interview with Odd himself."

"Of course." Drew said, rubbing his head as he tried not to scream. He realized sourly that this was only going to get worse. Now that he had let that little bit out, every interview was going to take a little bit more. Odd wasn't going to like this at all.

CHAPTER 20

"I don't know what's going on here, but it feels like bad karma."

–Zack Erikson

"Please, Lysander, you have to listen to me." Arlen chirped, following with a squeak that felt like somebody had jabbed Lysander in the ear. Lysander shivered, then angrily turned, accidently stepping on his keyboard.

He scowled, "I have listened. You've been telling me for months about how this Fallon is supposed to be after me. He still hasn't shown up."

"That's because he was waiting to see if you would stop. —*Eep!*— I wasn't supposed to warn you, either."

"Why did you?"

Arlen frowned, looking behind nervously at the dark sky, "I was just trying to be nice."

"Whatever." Lysander said sarcastically, frowning and turning to his computer. He had work to do.

Arlen wasn't leaving, "He has to act tonight, Lysander."

"Why's that?"

"We hibernate tonight. Just before morning." Arlen said.

"So that's why you've been acting so lazy." Lysander said, almost to himself. Arlen had been flying low, he had noticed.

And sometimes he even snuck off to do other things, like hunt for bugs. Why couldn't he do that later? He got more sleep than Lysander. Lysander scowled. He never got any sleep anymore. He would love to, but it just wasn't possible. He had to keep working. Lysander added, "What am I supposed to do when you hibernate, then? How am I supposed to talk to Drew?"

"I don't know… Maybe you could use the shouting machine." Arlen pointed to the cell phone. Lysander sighed. Arlen had been calling it the shouting machine ever since Lysander had tried to explain what it did.

"I don't want to use that, I have to maintain my distance… I might have to use e-mail." Lysander said.

"E-mail?" Arlen said, and then turned as if something had poked him. He stared outside the cave.

"What?" Lysander asked, looking past Arlen into the cave. He saw nothing.

Arlen whispered softly, "I thought I heard something. *Chee!*"

Lysander sighed and shook his head, "Okay, whatever. Here's the point. I'm going to need you to do a bunch of things, especially now that you're leaving me to hibernate. I've got three letters to be delivered to Drew, two of them on his porch but the third, this one," Lysander pointed to the top letter in the stack, "Has to be on his desk in the computer store."

"I *hate* going into that store." Arlen said, "They have those glass eyes… cameras, you called them. What if they see me?"

"You're a bat, they don't care too much about you. Besides, we left the grate open just to let you in all the time, so there isn't any problem."

Arlen bowed his head, the cloth around his eyes sagging slightly, showing burned tissue underneath, "Okay."

"After that, you need to fly around town, and tell me what places are still farmland so that they can be developed—" Lysander stopped. Arlen had flinched, almost cringing away from the cave entrance. He looked down the cave, squeaking a little.

"What now?" Lysander said, but then noticed it. It was the sound of flapping wings. The chorus of squeaking had the noise of some far-off, high-pitched storm.

"It's Fallon. Oh no, *chirk!*" Arlen chirped, peeking out to squeak as he did so, "There's at least ten, *chee!*"

"Out of my way." Lysander said, frustrated. Did the entire world want to stop him? He was trying to help these bats! He shoved past Arlen, muttering, "Like bats could hurt anybody." He stepped out into the twilight, looking around for the bats.

"Yeah?" A voice grunted. Lysander looked to the side where it had come from, but was blinded by the sun glaring in his eyes. Something smashed into him, sending him tumbling. Lysander scuffled, trying to regain his footing, but claws dug into his side, yanking him and sending him tumbling down the hill. The world turned into a whirlwind of color, his burned ear smacking the ground and sending a shock across his skull.

Then he hit a rock and stopped. His body screamed for mercy, Lysander grimly remembering how fragile his bones were. He might even have broken a rib. Not good. This couldn't happen now.

Lysander moved to his feet, but kept his eyes closed, feeling the different burning pains across his body. He analyzed the pain with cold calculation, searching for the type, the intensity. None of it stood out, and certainly a broken rib would have flared like fire. He was fine. Or at least not too horrible. He opened his eyes, facing upwards.

Fallon stood at the head of a dozen bats. His eyes were

squinted tightly shut against the sun, his mouth a thin, cruel line, "Am I so pathetic now? Or should we toss your body off another hill, pal?"

"You don't want to start this." Lysander said. He dimly registered Arlen in the background, chirping meekly. Mirada was also there, probably on the way to his cave when he had come out. Her mouth was open, a pile of uprooted plants at her feet.

"Look, pal." Fallon fluttered down to Lysander's eye level, "I heard you've been throwing your weight around. Being the boss. Well, I got a little weight. Every bat on this mountain is under my command. Yeah, we're not as big as you, but we have the numbers. We have what we need."

"You can't threaten me." Lysander said, tilting his head to display the black mark he knew was there, "I survived lightning. I escaped the humans, and I faced down a fox. Do you really think you can fight me?"

"I could kill you right now." Fallon hissed, "But I'll give you one chance. Beg for mercy, and I'll let you live, as long as you apologize to my brother and let him free, and stop what you're doing."

"Your brother?" Lysander cocked his head and thought for a second, "Oh, I get it."

Lysander hoisted himself higher, putting his nose right to Fallon's, "You're a brave one. But Arlen owes me his life. He'll repay me until the day he dies! And there's not a single thing you can do to stop that!"

"You're missing something." Fallon said. There was a sound at the edge of Lysander's hearing, like a screech. Fallon continued, "Arlen's a good bat, and he'll repay you. But if you're not there anymore, then Arlen can't really repay, can he?"

Lysander glared, "So you're going to fight me? You can't win that fight, not by yourself. And having your friends help doesn't really go with that honor system you bats love, now does it?"

"No, which is why I had to learn your lesson." Fallon said. Lysander turned. That sound was a screech. It had to be. He sniffed, but only got the scent of the river water.

Lysander asked, "What lesson?"

"You say a machine is something we use to do a job for us. I brought a machine." Fallon looked up as there was another humongous screech, "Scatter!"

The bats blew past Lysander like a black whirlwind, spreading in every direction. Lysander turned, trying to see what the screeching was. Just over the treetops, he glimpsed a bat fluttering like crazy, before zipping down into the trees. Then something else crested the treetops.

"Hawk!" Mirada screamed, ducking inside the cave. The black shape spread its wings against the sun, and then suddenly twisted into a dive. Lysander bolted, feet slipping before finally gaining traction and launching himself forward. His heart, already pounding, hurtled to the speed of a hummingbird's wing. He went straight for his cave, where a terrified Mirada peeked out. Arlen was gone, flying as fast as he could somewhere else.

He wasn't going to make it.

Lysander braked, throwing his whole body against the ground in a mad skid a foot away from the cave. His bruises screamed, the pain arcing to an entirely new level. The ground in front of the cave exploded, the hawk skipping off and taking to the air again, it's near success foiled by Lysander's sudden turn. Before it was even a dozen feet up, it spiraled down again, claws open in deadly hooks of muscle and claw.

Lysander tried to analyze the situation, but the impending death was making it difficult to concentrate. His adrenaline firing like a machine gun, he leapt to the side, scrambling under a root. Screeching so loud it made Lysander cringe, the hawk aborted the attack, landing a few feet away. Lysander shook, stepping back as the hawk spread its wings and let out a victory scream, charging forward. In his condition, Lysander knew that he couldn't run fast enough to escape. And the root only provided protection from aerial attack.

So Lysander charged. He took two hops forward, gulping and forcing his vocal cords open wider, make his voice lower. And then, stepping into human speech, he roared, "Feather-brain!"

The bird screamed, braking. Lysander knew its shock was only temporary. He had to keep going. He jumped forward, right into the path of the skidding bird talons. Then he opened his mouth, twisting sideways and biting as hard as he could.

It tasted disgusting. The hawk let out something between a screech and a gurgle, going into spasms. The claws closed, one cutting Lysander's leg. He kept his teeth clamped around the bird's leg, until his whole body was turned upside down. The bird snapped at him, its beak biting off a lot of fur and some stuff beneath. He gasped, letting go as his body was launched through the air. He felt the ground smash him twice, and then the world stopped heaving. There was a rustle of wings, and Lysander gritted his eyes, waiting for the sting of claws. But the flapping grew distant. The bird was running away.

CHAPTER 21

"Sometimes the cruelest thing we can do is just completely ignore somebody. That kind of torture can be worse than anything else."

–Lysander

Mirada shivered in the cold fall air. A horrible, trembling wind shook its way down the canyon, stirring the river and chilling Mirada to the bone. The river was still a little warm, but Mirada couldn't go down there right now. She was guarding the cave, waiting for Lysander to tell her what to do next. She had liked it at first. With Arlen hibernating, Lysander had needed help. Not just for food now, but also to guard the cave so Lysander wouldn't be disturbed. But as the days went by, Mirada began to hate the job. She wanted to talk to Lysander, but now she was trying to stop disturbances, and talking would be the opposite. Mirada, as much as she hated it, was talking to Lysander less than ever.

He was just too busy. All day long he worked on that machine, the glowing rectangle and little square 'buttons' that Mirada still didn't understand. He limped around the cave, bearing injuries somewhere under his skin from the hawk attack, but never letting on. His cut on his leg had healed, and the patch of missing fur looked okay, if rather ugly. Some would say he was just fine. Mirada could tell, though. Every time he

clicked a button, she could see him twitch a little, as if the movement hurt him. Despite all of that, he kept going. The pain just seemed to fuel his need to be on the machine. He was doing something with the humans, that much she knew. Somehow, Lysander had told her, he was going to get revenge.

Of course, Mirada told herself, Lysander would never do that. He must have meant something different from what it sounded like, that was all. Lysander was too nice to do something like that. Of course, Lysander had been acting strange again. He was doing that thing where he stared off into space, or worked so hard he ignored everything else. That wasn't good for him, and Mirada didn't like it one bit. Right now, she was trying to think of ways to make him stop. He would thank her; she was only doing it for his own good.

"Mirada?" A voice crossed her thoughts. Mirada looked up, seeing Tysell. Mirada tried not to wrinkle her nose, though the instinct was immediate. Tysell hated when she did that.

"Hi, Ty." Mirada said.

"Does he know your real name now?" Tysell gestured with her head at the cave.

Mirada sighed, "No. Still calls me Mira. If he calls me at all."

Tysell nodded sadly. They sat in an awkward silence for a second, one of the first Mirada had with Tysell. Before they had talked all the time. But they hadn't done anything together in so long that it had become awkward between them. Mirada had been too busy. Now she had to find food for two people, after all. Tysell was always off somewhere else, just trying to find enough food for herself. Mirada used to help her with that, before she had gotten too busy. Now that didn't really happen, and without their food-finding time, the two barely even saw each other anymore.

Tysell finally broke the silence, "You should come inside. It's cold."

"Can't. I have to… make sure no one gets in, I guess. And I think he's going to be hungry soon…"

"How are you getting food for him?"

Mirada smiled, "I made a big food store in my cave, bigger than usual. I'm using a lot of that. But I still have to find food."

"Y'know, I don't think that's fair." Tysell said, moving over to Mirada, who instinctively leaned away, "You ain't getting enough food anymore."

Mirada shrugged.

"Why d'you do that? You do it all?" Tysell asked, "I know you… *like* him, but still."

Mirada was silent, trying to figure out how to explain, but couldn't find the exact words. She shivered in the cold wind, smelling winter coming. Looking at Tysell, she sighed, "I guess I just have to make him notice me. However long it takes. That doesn't make sense, does it? I guess you can't understa—"

Mirada cut herself short, but it was too late. Tysell's face was frozen in place. Slowly, Tysell looked away.

Mirada inwardly hit herself, "You know I didn't mean it that way."

"But it's true." Tysell said, "No matter what you meant."

"Tysell, it's okay that you're not… um…"

"Not perfect? Can't smell, can't talk good." Tysell grimaced, "Dirty fur, dirty breath, broken tooth." She grinned crookedly to illustrate, flaming red gums where the piece was missing, one of her center teeth.

Mirada flinched as Tysell sneezed violently.

"Besides, you're wrong." Tysell's voice was oddly playful, out of tone, "I actually got someone that does got a thing for me."

"Who…" Mirada frowned, squinting as she thought. Then, her eyes snapped wide. Mirada gasped, "Not… not *Darshep?*"

Tysell grinned her sideways grin. It had to be Darshep, Mirada now realized. He was always near Tysell, somehow. He scavenged by her, sat next to her in a crowd. When Tysell had a bad day finding food, which was somewhat often, there was always food in her burrow. Mirada had thought Tysell had saved it, but realized that Tysell never found enough food to save anything. Someone had put it there, and now it was obvious who. Darshep's burrow also happened to be very close to Tysell's which Mirada doubted was merely a coincidence.

"Tysell, that's wonderful!" Mirada announced, completely forgetting about being quiet, "See, even you, um… I mean."

"Yeah, even me." Tysell scowled, huffing a wave of putrid air, "You just can't stop, huh?"

"Sorry." Mirada cringed.

Tysell turned away.

"I didn't mean it. Besides, if he already likes you it doesn't matter… right?" Mirada said tentatively. Tysell sniffed, and then sneezed.

Sniffing again, Tysell sobbed, "I want to be like you. I ain't good enough, you are! You're perfect and all, and Darshep is our leader. I'm the freaky dirty bunny. How's *that* supposed to work? Darshep and me just don't match, see."

"Ty…" Mirada sighed. She moved up to Tysell, forcing herself to sit right up to her, despite the dirt, "It's okay."

Tysell sniffed.

Mirada slowly said, her voice inviting, "You know, the river is still pretty warm. A bath could get off all that dirt, no matter how much. Plus, if you smile a certain way, that tooth won't show, see? And down the river, there's some mint leaves. You could chew those, and rub up against the patch of flowers by them. That would make you smell *really* nice."

"Mirada, I can't smell." Tysell said before gasping a huge, tear sodden breath.

"I know *you* can't." Mirada said, "But Darshep can."

Tysell looked over, face streaked with tears, "Oh, Mirada…"

That was it. That was all Tysell needed to turn around and forgive Mirada for everything she had done, for all the abuse Mirada had put her through. That was why they had used to be friends. Mirada needed Tysell's strength, and Tysell needed Mirada's talent. For good or bad, they were together forever.

"Come on." Mirada said, leading Tysell slowly down the bank to the river. Odd would be fine by himself for a few seconds.

"That's what friends are for, right?"

CHAPTER 22

"I swear, whoever that Odd person is, he must have like, 50 hours a day or something. Because even if I had 100 hours a day, I still couldn't do what he does."

–Zack Erikson

Drew was in his home office, night falling, when the phone rang. He looked at the caller-ID, and hesitated. Odd didn't call. He e-mailed now, not a single letter, and not a single call. Drew pressed the answer button, "Hello?"

"I'm not very happy with you." Odd said.

Sarcastically, Drew noted how Odd always got straight to the point.

Odd continued, "I just saw something on the internet news. It was an article about you. You and me."

Drew grimaced. Of course, Odd would have had to find out eventually. Drew was surprised he hadn't learned about it way before now. Was he completely oblivious to the outside world? Apparently, he was nearly so.

"I'm sorry." Drew began, "I just..." His voice dropped into a whisper, but he couldn't go on. He leaned onto his desk, resting his arms on the printer.

"You promised. I gave you all you have, and barely asked anything in return. A cell phone, letting me keep the computer I stole. Not telling anyone about me." Odd sounded hurt,

emotionally bitten. A croaky edge to his voice suggested that he might not be so well off physically, either.

"I didn't mean to."

"Then how did it happen?" Odd's voice was dripping acid, "Complete betrayal isn't an everyday thing, you know."

"You asked me to talk to those reporters!"

"To talk about what *you* were doing, what you were selling. You were never supposed to mention me." Odd breathed a quick, short breath, like he was trying to hold in his anger.

Drew waved an arm in frustration, "They ask so many questions! It just slipped out, it wasn't my fault."

"You can't control your own tongue? What are you, a blabbering five-year-old?" Odd's word ripped into Drew, "Haven't you realized I don't like popularity? Haven't you gotten a hint that maybe I have a reason to stay secret?"

Drew gulped, trying to force out an answer. It seemed like every single sentence Odd said was taking a piece of him, leaving a little less behind to fight with. He mumbled, "What reason?"

"Oh, you'd love me to tell you that, wouldn't you? That way you could have something else to pass on to the world. Why don't you go ahead and record this call, Drew? Post it on the internet for everyone to see. You could turn me over to the cops, have them track me by my phone."

The thought had occurred to Drew before. He shook his head, "Look, pal. I'm sorry, okay? I can't do anything to fix what's happened. But if you're so smart, why don't you think of something yourself? You're so great at giving me orders, think up another little plan!"

Odd paused, and hissed, "You think it's really that easy? How am I supposed to stop the whole world, Drew? You think

I can stop all those reporters, just hold them off and never let them bother you again? You've been giving them all these little tidbits, telling all these little pieces you know about me. How are they going to like it when you just cut them off?"

Drew buried his head in his arms, "Whatever. Just leave me alone, okay? I should just hang up. Jess doesn't like me talking to you anyway." He used Jess as an excuse, hoping that the memory of her stern personality and demanding nature might rub off on him just by thinking of her. That way, he might be able to fight Odd a little bit. It didn't help, though. Drew was ready to promise anything to make Odd stop insulting him.

Odd snapped at him again, "Your wife? I thought she wanted you to be a success, Drew. What have I made you?"

Drew didn't answer, chills running down his spine. How did Odd know about Jess? He laid the phone down on the printer, turning away. But it was so quiet in the house. Jess and the kids had gone to a play. He had been too busy to go. Odd's voice, quiet as it was on the phone, was perfectly audible.

"Look, listen to me."

Drew reached for the phone automatically, and then pulled back. He could just leave it, or say he couldn't hear Odd. He could even hang up. Either of them could end the conversation, but Drew knew that he would never be able to go through with that, especially not with Odd on the line.

Drew numbly picked up the phone.

"For now, you'll just have to tell them… that I'm considering talking. Maybe I'll talk, but probably not. If, I say *if*, I think of something, I'll tell you. But until then, do the job I wanted you to do in the first place.

"This is what happens, Drew, when you don't listen to me."

Drew grew angry enough to actually say something, "I figured that out, thanks. So what else can I do for the great and wonderful Odd?"

"You can cut the sarcasm." Odd snipped.

Drew bit his lip.

Odd sighed, "You know, I would love to say this is a horrible surprise. That I could have never seen you betraying my trust like that. But to be honest, I always knew this would happen." The phone clicked, the line dead.

And a short distance away, Lysander smiled in the glow of his own phone, "In fact, I hoped it would."

CHAPTER 23

"I don't understand lots of stuff. But it's still real. Just because I'm stupid doesn't mean stuff is going to be simple."

–Zack Erikson

"Thanks for having me today, Mr. Howell." The reporter said as he shook Drew's hand and sat down in the small office chair. He looked uncomfortable, out of place away from his big TV studio.

Drew smiled, "I'm glad you could fly in." He took a seat behind his desk.

"Oh, I wouldn't miss today. So, this is one of the factories. Even comes with your own office." The reporter grinned, "You've been building quite a few factories lately. And in such a small town. Unusual for a business like yours. Of course, your business is hardly usual."

"Yes…I suppose so." Drew agreed.

"But let's get down to business. Your business. Drew, all these factories make one thing, and one thing only. A computer. You only have a single model, and a consumer would have to purchase a screen and keyboard from other companies. A rather unusual setup, for such massive sales. It's mostly due to your advertisements, which use the following line. I quote:" The reporter held up a clipboard dramatically, "Twice as fast,

twice as easy, twice as awesome… half the cost."

"That would be the line, yes." Drew said, not knowing what he was supposed to say, as usual. Still, he was getting better at interviews, which was good because they were coming more and more frequently. At least in the interviews, the interviewer would smile and be friendly, which helped Drew's confidence. He often stared at the reporter's smile, instead of his eyes. They didn't seem to notice.

The reporter picked up the slack, "Several companies reviewing your product confirm that those claims are true. But the question everyone is wondering Drew, is how? We have no explanation. Of course, other companies are probably reverse-engineering as we speak, but so far we've heard nothing."

"Good luck to them." Drew grinned, "They're going to have a bit of trouble. It doesn't work like most computers."

"How does it work?"

"Well, I brought one here for demonstration." Drew said, pulling across a black box towards him on the otherwise empty desk. He still hadn't moved in. Drew smiled as wide as he could, though it was beginning to hurt, "Not the prettiest thing ever, I think it looks like a big black brick. But we're working on design. Here, look." He popped off the top of the computer, and flipped it upright so the insides were visible to the camera, "Looks normal, mostly. At least at first. But here's the piece that makes it different."

Drew reached in around the box awkwardly, grabbing a piece and pulling until it finally popped out of its socket. He unplugged all the wires that led to it, and held it up, not realizing it obscured his face from the camera, "This is it."

He held a large computer chip, about the size of his hand. It was shaped as a large triangle, which divided into smaller and smaller triangles, sparkling with a shimmer of blue, purple, and green, "The whole computer is made of things like these."

"That doesn't look much like a piece of a computer. Looks like something I'd see on a science-fiction movie." The reporter said, "Why does it look like that? Triangular, I mean."

"Well, it begins with binary. You know how computers are based on 0's and 1's? That's how every computer runs."

"Okay…?" The reporter's tone begged more information.

"Everything a computer does is from those two numbers. 1 is on and 0 is off. A switch. In a computer, there are piles and piles of switches, and every time you press a button, you fire off dozens and dozens of them in a huge chain reaction, which causes your computer to do what it should do."

"Right." The reporter said, "So I assume Odd's computer does this faster, somehow."

Drew frowned, "Yes and no. See, he added a 2. So 1 is on, 0 is off, and 2 is… maybe. Or hot, cold, and warm, if that makes more sense. White, black, and grey. So now to get to a destination, the data has three paths to take instead of two, meaning less switches are needed. See, a two-way path leads to two more two-way paths, which makes four destinations. But a three-way path leading to three different other three-way paths makes nine. It only took two switches, but there are more than double the possibilities. Except the differences are a lot bigger than that. There are thousands of switches in a computer, and that adds up to make a huge difference. Less switches needed means less time needed. We can use less, and do so much more with it."

"Added to Odd's amazing software, which makes it even better. A computer that instantly adapts to be the computer you want it to be."

"Yes." Drew nodded, placing the chip gently on the computer, "I think this is why he called our product line the Triangle System. He was planning to release this."

"Triangle System, indeed, but why the name of the company? *Bunny Computers*, I think it's called."

"No idea on that one." Drew shrugged, "Odd's idea."

"I'm certain Odd has a lot of ideas. Our viewers are extremely curious to what some of those might be. Though I hear today we have a treat."

"Yes." Drew smiled, "Today, Odd's going to talk to everyone, on a live telephone call. He'll be giving a dedicatory speech for this new factory we're in."

"Well, viewers, keep tuned, because that's coming right up."

CHAPTER 24

"I know how to do public speaking. All I have to do is talk for a really, really long time, and make sure I don't say anything."

–Drew Howell

Drew didn't even have to say a word. That is, if he could have drummed up the courage to say anything in the first place. The mass of reporters nearly blinded him with camera snaps, flashes bursting like lifeless white bombs and clicks going off like machine guns. He scratched the microphone, and it came clearly over the speakers. He had meant it as a sound test, but a few people winced at the unnatural noise. Camera flashes seemed to surge, cameramen flinching from the noise and taking photos by accident.

Drew moved to the back of the stage, and sat down in the only chair. At least he didn't have to do anything for these few minutes. He had barely gotten a moment's rest lately, even for sleep. His kids were noticing, and complained. He felt horrible, but what could he do? Everyone expected him to do everything, especially Odd. At least Odd had told him to get assistants. People to file his paperwork, taxes, all the tasks that took time but not authority. Drew should have thought of getting assistants. He felt like he wasn't thinking at all anymore.

Drew sighed, turning in his chair and nodding. One of

his new assistants, a computer tech just out of college, nodded back and then started working on the back-stage equipment. The stage had been erected just in front of the new factory. That is, if you could call it a stage. The gravel bed that was left had been flattened into a raised platform, speakers plopped down wherever was most convenient at the moment. Folding chairs bought in bulk a week before were lined up in neat rows in front of the gravel, completely full. Wires dragged over it all, and a podium borrowed from the elementary school was in front, leaning a little in the gravel. Finally the tech seemed to be ready. He looked at Drew questioningly, who nodded again. Finally he flipped the switch.

There was a slight crackle, like someone picking up a phone. Then some sort of scuffling sound.

Odd's voice came over the speakers, "If you can hear me, could you raise your hands?"

Most of the reporters responded. The voice seemed to grin happily, almost cheekily as it said, "Good! My name's Odd. You might have heard of me."

There was some polite chuckling. Odd's voice continued, coming through clearer than Drew had ever heard, but still with that same, accent-free voice of a con man. To Drew, it had first been inviting, then friendly, and finally extremely demanding. To them it was enthusiastic, happy, carefree.

Drew was beginning to hate that voice.

"I think it's just great how excited everyone is over my computers! I mean, it's nice to see that something I worked so hard on is actually becoming useful in the world."

There were murmurs, and a few reporters began to stand up, yelling questions. Odd cut them off, "Not right now! Give me a chance to explain before we do that. And we're not doing it in the normal way, either."

The reporters quieted.

"Of course, I hardly do things in a normal way. I guess that's partly why I'm becoming so famous. One of the best ways to get somebody to want to know something is to not tell them what it is. You have no idea, no facts about me, no personal information."

Odd took a breath, and continued, "You came here today for answers. I guess I should give you a few. So here's some fun facts about yours truly; I don't remember much of my childhood, due to an event that nearly took my life. I haven't ever eaten meat, I was born with white hair, and I lived in the same town as Drew my whole life. There, a few clues. But I promise they won't help you find out who I am. Not because I lied! Just because I have a great deal of privacy. Not many people have even seen me face to face."

The reporters' pens scribbled as they took frantic notes, but Odd wasn't slowing, "I really enjoy my privacy. I love it. Almost as much as I love making computers. That's where the problem is. Your computers are very open things. At least, they seem to be. A person's whole life story can be out there on the internet for everyone to see.

"But what if that person lied? It's really hard to figure out lying on the internet. You could put a picture of someone much younger than you, or say you have a job as CEO instead of janitor. You could lie about where you live, even your gender. So here's the question: why do you want to know so much about me, if I can lie so easily?"

Drew frowned. What was Odd playing at? He was supposed to use this interview to make people stop asking questions, not make them suspicious.

Odd's voice, after the perfectly timed pause, said, "Look, I'm not asking you to do something you wouldn't normally do. I make things. I'm like an engineer, I build a computer like an architect builds a good building. You walk in buildings every day, but you never ask who made them. Is that person trustworthy? How do you even know that architect was trained? The entire building could collapse on your pretty little heads, and yet you don't worry. You can see in a glance the building was built well. Just like everyone sees my computers. They see they work, they live up to every high expectation and more."

Odd took a deep breath, "So can I ask a favor? Back off. Stop asking questions. Respect my privacy. I gave total ownership to Drew, I didn't take anything for myself. All because I don't want to be in the limelight. So can we agree to let things stay as they are? Can you please stop asking questions you know I can't answer, and let me get to work for you? Every second I have to protect myself from your questions is precious seconds I'm not inventing. And I have a lot of ideas I want to use. Sound fair?"

There was murmuring, somewhat discontent, but calmed, like a pool that was disturbed, but ripples slowly fading. Odd added, "Of course, you all have a job. You guys ask questions. I want my privacy, but since you're so insistent… I'm going to do you all a favor. I'll let a single reporter ask a single question. Think hard about what you want. And the reporter I want to ask it is named Cory Yalk. He says he's the expert on me, so I figured he'd be the obvious choice."

The ripples seemed to be growing. The reporters were angrily whispering, obviously discontent that they couldn't ask, that they were being told what to do by a voice they couldn't see. But then one stood up. Drew recognized him as Cory Yalk.

He had been the one who had first said Odd might be a hacker. Drew still wasn't sure how he felt about that. He was certain that if Odd wanted, he could be a hacker, but that didn't necessarily mean he *was* one, after all.

At least Drew hoped that was the case.

Cory said loudly, above the noise, "You haven't told us much today, Odd. And I'm sure this is like those three wish stories. I ask something, and you twist it so that I don't get what I want. A challenge. So, this is my question."

He waited, just like Odd would have, until the crowd was completely silent. Then, with a rather normal voice, he asked, "What are you afraid of?"

The microphone was silent. Then, there was a huge click, so loud Drew flinched. He waited, listening breathlessly for the answer. It didn't come. The crowd began to talk, getting louder. Drew looked to the side at his assistants. The one on the switches was frantically flipping buttons, like something was wrong. Drew got up, walking as fast as he could without breaking into a run.

He grabbed the guy, pulling him away from the switches and ripping the headphones off his head, "What's wrong, what's going on here?"

"I can't be certain… but it looks… looks like…"

"Like what?"

"Odd hung up."

Drew gaped, looking back into the crowd. Standing like a rock amidst the rising noise, Cory Yalk wore a fat, satisfied grin.

CHAPTER 25

"Even smart dudes are stupid if they're angry. You can't think and scream at the same time."

–Zack Erikson

Cory Yalk's phone rang no less than a dozen times before he finally arrived at the hotel. He chuckled as it began to ring again, parking his car and slowly walking up to his room. *No distractions while driving!* He thought to himself sarcastically. Instead he listened to the sound of crickets chirping away in the dead-dry Utah air. Utah weather was very unusual. It had been hot, but when he started sweating the other day his sweat actually cooled him off. He was used to big cities by the coast, where the muggy air would make your clothes wet before you even had a chance to sweat. Then the cold days, wind blowing over the ocean and never relenting. Here the air hung around him, crisping hotter and hotter without a breeze in sight. He was only thankful for the night. The only sounds in the world now were the low rumble of cars and his relentless phone. He still didn't answer.

The real reason he didn't answer was that he wanted to let it stew by itself, a nice roast frying in a pressure cooker. Cory prided himself on his question. He wasn't sure what was going to happen, but he was certain it was going to work. The plan,

whatever that was, was going perfectly. All he had to do was decide what it was.

Cory was a reporter, sure. But he liked it when his information came to him. And sometimes, he found, it wasn't quite cooked enough. So he'd rather let it boil for a bit.

He sat down in his room, overlooking the highway. Delivery convoys from the factories crawled up the onramps. White noise and the biting smell of oil rose from the highway, only slightly muffled by the cheap hotel walls.

He checked the call list. Several were from his employers, probably asking if he had gone mad and itching to fire him. Stay out of it, they would say. Don't get involved, you should never ever do that. Cory knew that to catch the dirtier crooks you were going to have to get a little dirty yourself. Some calls were from reporters, most likely spitting mad or wondering about his thoughts, wanting to steal his opinions. A low way of writing, but most news was secondhand. Even Cory's stories. Actually, Cory hadn't written a single story at all. A lot of stories listed his name as the author, of course, but he had no time to write them himself. Not enough time. There was one number Cory didn't recognize.

He was interrupted as the phone began to ring again in his hands, playing out some elevator music. Cory didn't like the ringtone, but he loved the attention it got if other people were around. It was the mystery number.

Cory answered, "A little steamed, Odd?"

"What do you want?" Odd's voice hissed angrily, rather high-pitched, "What kind of question is that, anyway?"

"It wasn't actually a question." Cory said, smiling and closing his eyes as he leaned back in his chair. He had been frantically trying to find out about Odd, trying to get contact

with him since he had first known about his existence. At the moment, he had people scanning the internet for traces of him, connections. Now Odd was in his field, and Cory wasn't going to let him out without a fight.

"What exactly was it supposed to be? Sounded like a question."

"*It* sounded like a question." Cory said, holding up a finger even though Odd couldn't see, "Grammer, my friend."

Odd was silent, but Cory could just register the sound of heavy, almost frantic breathing. Was Odd hyperventilating?

"That question I asked at the interview wasn't one I wanted an answer to. I knew you wouldn't answer a question like that."

"Then why did you ask it?"

Cory shook his head, like he was lecturing a child, and said with a smile, "I wanted the answer, but not for me. I just wanted you to think of it. I wanted to provoke you, get a little real emotion that so far, I haven't seen a bit of."

Cory waited for an answer, but when the silence stretched on, he leaned forward in his chair, "You know what it tells me when you don't answer, Odd? It means I was right."

"No!"

"Well, you haven't said I was wrong."

"Look!" There was the scuffling of a phone being shifted, a sound like something scraping on dirt, "I'm not scared of anything!"

"Finally, I'm getting something here. Some emotion. Fear, and lots of it."

"What would I have to be afraid of? You can't say a single thing that scares me!" Odd's voice challenged.

Cory stood up, almost spitting into the phone, "Me.

You're scared of me."

Odd's voice quivered, "…What is wrong with you?"

"I could ask you the same thing." Cory said, "What do you even want, Odd?"

"I told everyone at the press conference that—"

"Yeah, I know." Cory cut Odd off, beginning to pace across the room. He was getting sweaty. He turned the thermostat down but then back again, guessing it wasn't the temperature. Cory shook his head as he spoke, "I actually was a psychology minor, did you know that? Journalism major, Psychology and Computer Technology minors. A whole pile of degrees, actually. What I heard wasn't a shy little nerd who just wanted to sit around and program computers. That thing back there was a prepared, formulated speech. Pauses, reasoning to get them on your side, polite requests. You know how to work a crowd."

"I got lucky."

"Lucky or not, you had talent. You know about people. You know how to make them do what you want. Rabble-rousing, I call it. Yet you said you hate the limelight."

"I do." Odd said, though his voice was now less angry. But the quick, frantic breathing was still there. Cory went over and leaned on the side of the window.

Cory said, "Didn't you say that the best way to get attention is to act like you don't want it?"

After a pause, Odd sighed, "That is what I said. You are very smart, Mr. Yalk."

"*Mr.* Yalk. So you respect me?"

"Very observant, too."

"You act like you've lost some kind of contest!" Cory said, grinning, "Don't feel too bad! You're smarter than me. It's just

that I don't always need to be smart. I was lucky enough to stumble across your weakness. You hate losing, and I made you feel like you lost. Then you began to come apart."

"I expected you to listen to me like everyone else." Odd said, "But I see you're going to be a bit more difficult than that."

"I hope I am." Cory said, "Can I ask you a question?"

"Of course. But I might not answer."

"What do you really want?"

Odd chuckled, "Mr. Yalk, you really are a piece of work. I guess you deserve an answer. I'll tell you, because no one would believe it after my speech today. My real desire is quite simple. I want revenge."

The phone clicked as Odd hung up. Cory pulled it off his face and frowned. He felt like Odd must have, after Cory had asked the impossible question. Cory shook his head, "I'm sorry I asked."

CHAPTER 26

"Chicks take everything the wrong way. If one ever asks you if she's fat, well… you're pretty much doomed no matter what you say."

–Zack Erikson

Mirada wondered what was wrong with her. She was almost sick of asking herself that, but she had to. She had thought maybe Lysander was too involved in whatever he did on that computer machine, but that wasn't it. He was always clicking buttons and sometimes talking in that little thing in the human voice, which scared her. It was obviously pointless, but it was also plainly obvious that it was the most exciting thing he had to do. Therefore, Mirada was worse than absolute boredom. She was torture. That was the only explanation.

It was something with her. But what? Not her grooming. Mirada was always clean, always incredibly clean. In fact, as she sat there in the freezing cold, just inside Lysander's cave, she was cleaning herself again. It was instinct now, something she did as she was thinking. It didn't even matter that as soon as she licked herself, the spit would freeze on her fur, and she'd have to lick it again and again just to stop her entire body from turning into an ice sheet.

Maybe it was her attitude. She tried to be happy, but Lysander wasn't happy very often. And when he was happy,

his face was almost… scary. Like he was plotting. He never laughed at her jokes, either, and if she talked too much he would promptly ask her to leave. He never tried anything new. That of course, was normal. Extremely so. A classic survival instinct, hiding from any danger and refusing to come out for any reason. All bunnies did that. But it frustrated Mirada. She knew that he should notice her. She wasn't scary or anything. At least, she didn't mean to be.

But what use was it thinking about that? She was still sitting here, on the frozen ground peeking out of a burrow hole, craning her neck to see Lysander's. Luckily she was no longer on guard duty. Lysander was actually annoyed by the sound of her breathing and told her she wasn't needed anymore. That had really hurt.

Of course, she could just ask.

No, that was pathetic. Mirada saw it in her mind now, walking in to Lysander's burrow, something that always annoyed him. Then as he turned, annoyed at the interruption, she would ask, 'Hey, so I'm obsessed with you, but you hate me. Why is that?'

It just wouldn't work.

That is, it wouldn't work normally. But then, Lysander wasn't normal. Mirada knew that Lysander was unlikely to remember awkward conversations, even though he remembered everything else. And he didn't understand implications, he only saw the obvious. In a way, he saw better than anyone else, but had no peripheral vision. He missed anything that wasn't right in front of him.

Mirada thought, formulating her question for an eternity. Finally, with her heart thrumming like a tiny car, she booked it across the snow. Her feet skid, kicking up a plume several feet high as she struggled to gain traction. Every predator within a mile would have noticed that. But in only seconds Mirada was already safe inside Lysander's hole.

"Who's that? I hope it's not you, Mira." Lysander's annoyed voice echoed out. There was another weird sound, too, like a mixture of water, thumping, bird tweets and low moans. Something about it made Mirada very happy. She didn't know why. And it was quiet, too. Mirada hadn't heard it at all in the other hole, even with her hearing.

"Lysander?" She called, "What are those noises?"

"Music. It's something humans invented." Lysander said as he came into the hole's hallway to look at her, "I'm listening to it so I can process why it's so popular."

"Oh, well... that's great." Mirada said. She smiled shyly.

Lysander waited. Then he raised an eyebrow, "Did you need something, or are you going to waste my time all day?"

"Oh! Um..." Mirada scratched herself quickly, and flinched inwardly. Scratching was hardly attractive. She said, "I just wanted to ask you something."

"Go ahead." Lysander said, a sigh mingling with the two words.

"There's this bunny, and I like him... so I was wondering what you... um... what would make me more attractive?" She smiled.

Lysander squinted, "Why do you want to be attractive to him?"

Mirada frowned, "You know, I like him."

"What? That's hardly a reason."

"I *really* like him." Mirada said.

Lysander blinked, "Oh! I see. And you want advice from me to make you more attractive?"

"Yes."

"And *then* you'll leave?"

Mirada bit her lip, "Yep."

"Well, what's he like?" Lysander asked.

Mirada said, "He's you. I mean, he's, um, like you! A *lot* like you! Well, not a lot, but he's sort of… um… he has white fur, and two eyes, that is, two eyes like your two eyes. Both the eyes are the same."

"Just because he looks like me doesn't mean he'll like the same things as me."

"Well, just… just tell me what you would like." Mirada said.

Lysander sighed, "Alright, but I can't guarantee anything."

"That's okay! That's great!"

"Look… well, you have clean fur, that's good, I guess. And a *lot* of fur." Lysander raised an eye, "A lot."

"I'm not fat… am I?"

"Well, all angora rabbits are naturally massive, and the long fur makes you appear even larger." Lysander said, "So yes, you are quite fat in appearance, even if you're in the normal weight range."

"Oh…" Mirada said, her frown deepening.

"And if you frown all the time he's going to think you're cynical." Lysander added.

"Sorry." Mirada said, and tried a weak smile. Her bottom lip quivered, but she was concentrating more on keeping her eyes dry, "What else?"

Lysander cocked his head to the side, "You don't look so good."

Mirada blinked, "What?"

Lysander took a step forward, looking at her closely, "You

okay? You look… stressed. Is it about this guy you like?" He seemed genuinely interested. Somehow, he had been drawn out of his obsession with machines again. He was different now.

"Yeah." Mirada admitted, "He's… hard to impress."

"Then maybe you should dump him."

Mirada opened her mouth, but had no idea what to say.

Lysander added, "You can't let this guy ruin your life, Mirada."

Mirada sighed, "It's just he's so… different. And very hard to be around. But sometimes he's different. He's… kind."

"I see." Lysander said, "A redeeming quality. I guess if that works for you."

Mirada grinned, though her eyes still felt wet, "It does."

Lysander thought, and then said, "Okay, some last advice. You tend to barge in on me a lot. If you, um, *like* this bunny, as you say, you probably barge in on him too, right?"

"Only sometimes." Mirada said.

"Good, because he'd probably just get annoyed if you did it as much as you do to me. When you do approach him, you have to get him to notice you, and being annoying isn't the way you want to do that."

Mirada felt herself nodding, but had to look away. She sniffed loudly. In a scratchy whisper, she asked, "So how do I make him notice?"

Lysander shrugged, "You could be honest and simply tell him, but if he doesn't return your feelings that would just be awkward."

"I don't think he does."

Lysander nodded, "Then I guess you just have to keep trying other ways."

"Okay." Mirada said, and sniffed a huge one, "Thank

you… for your help."

"I hope it works." Lysander said. Mirada nodded once to him and begin to hop slowly away. When she got out into the blinding white snow, she should have run, but didn't change her speed. If a predator wanted to eat her alive, let it.

"Mira?" Lysander asked.

She turned, hoping he'd mistake her wet cheeks for something else, "Yeah?"

"What's his name?"

Mirada opened her mouth, but then realized what the question was. She could say it, of course. Like Lysander said, it would be incredibly awkward. But at least he would know. There was no way he could see around that. It would be so obvious, so blatantly obvious. Normally, Mirada would have done it.

But today, she was done. She didn't want a single ounce more of pain than she had already brought. And to be fair, she wasn't good enough for Lysander anyway. So she turned her fat, cynical, annoying body, and lumbered away back to her hole without another word.

CHAPTER 27

"I just did what she wanted. Exactly what
she wanted. How can she hate that?"

–Drew Howell

"This is insanity!" Jess waved the printed e-mail in the air, "How can you even consider this?"

Drew moved around the couch, "It's an idea of Odd's—"

"Of course it is." Jess huffed, throwing the paper on the coffee table, "Everything is his idea. You don't think for yourself anymore."

"Well, my thinking never got us anywhere, did it?" Drew asked, "Just that pet store that you hated so much. That was never enough for you."

"Is that all you ever talk about?" Jess put her arms in the air, "I haven't heard the end of that sad old story since you closed it."

Drew turned away, folding his arms. The smell of burning was just beginning to drift from the kitchen, underlying the heat of his rage. She was never happy with what he did.

"Look. I love the computer store. It has better business, better service, it's much cleaner. But I don't understand this thing with Odd. You still don't know his real name. How can you even listen to him?"

"We're partners. Business partners."

Jess said, "You're not a partner, you're his slave! You do whatever he wants you to do."

Drew tried to keep his voice in check, "That's not true."

Jess waved at the phone set in the corner, "I picked that up the other day, and it just so happened that you were talking to Odd. I hear how he talks to you. He abuses you. No one else ever acts that way towards you."

"You do." Drew said. The air crystallized as the words hung. Jess's eyes narrowed, and she turned away, folding her arms.

Drew tried to explain, "I was just doing what you wanted. You wanted me to be something, actually do something with that business degree. Odd gave me a chance to do that. For you. I just wanted you to be happy about what I did. You've never been happy with me."

"That is what I said." Jess said. She sniffed softly, the sound ripping at Drew's heart. He sucked in a deep breath, which rattled on his dry lungs. His heart seemed to be trying to escape his chest.

Jess turned, a tear dripping from one eye and curling around her nose, "But I didn't want it this way."

"I don't understand."

"Drew... I've always pushed you. I've shoved. I wanted everything you had." Jess's voice was cracked, but still as strong as ever, "I saw you on a pillar, and that's where I wanted you. I wanted you to be the best, and so I pushed. But you know where you ended up? You ended up on top, but only because you've been hauled there by that freak you call Odd. He holds you on that pillar on a big old string of his. And you dance like his little puppet!"

Drew flinched.

"I don't want a puppet, Drew." Jess shook her head, "Maybe this is my fault, some. I pushed too much. I asked what you couldn't give. And so you sold yourself to that monster because he could give it. That'd make me happy with you, you thought."

Drew shook his head, "You're never happy."

"Wrong." Jess took a few steps forward, resting her hand on his shoulder, "I don't want you to be successful because of the *stuff* it gets. I want you to be successful because I know that you can do it. I want an amazing husband, dear. Not an amazing bank account."

Drew looked up, "It sure didn't sound that way to me."

"Then that's my fault, and I'm sorry." Jess said, resting her head in his arms, "I explained wrong, and you always thought that was the final call."

Drew smiled, laying his head down on her shoulder. For a while, they stood there, Drew trying to process what his wife had said. Had he been wrong this whole time?

Through all that bluster, all that forcing and demands, she had been trying to help him. Jess had always been the one to take charge. She had actually set up a lot of their dates, even dropped a few rather blunt hints that Drew should propose to her. Drew had even panicked during *that*, but Jess had helped him through. And during all those interviews and conferences with the press, hiring employees and talking to construction companies, she had been right there.

Not there in person, but still there.

Whenever Drew got nervous, wanted to run away or give up, she seemed to surface in his mind. She was always there, demanding more. He had borrowed her strength, asked him-

self what she would have done and then tried to do that. Sometimes it even worked. He would have gotten nowhere without her, Drew realized. Before she had come along, he was planning to drop out of college. He even had a job in place at a fast food joint. He had planned to stay in that job until he got too old to flip burgers. She had given him a second chance, and a will to make it into something.

Drew sighed, leaning down and scooping up the paper from the table. Jess broke her hold, taking a step back, but grabbed his hand in a secure grip. Almost like a handshake, but rather gentle for her.

"So what do we do, then?" Drew asked, "About this, I mean."

"Well, like I said, it's completely insane. It would never work, except... for him." Jess let out a deep breath, "Whoever he is, he knows what he's doing."

"And you don't think this is a little extreme?"

Jess smiled, "Of course it is. Just like my expectations."

Drew grinned, "I think I have an idea." He let go of her hand and walked over to the phone. His hands hit the speed dial for Odd's phone. He raised it, and waited. Slowly, he turned around to Jess. She had her arms folded, passive, waiting for him to do something.

"Odd? This is Drew. I've looked over your e-mail, and I think I can agree to it." Drew said, "That is, on a few conditions."

Jess smiled.

CHAPTER 28

"If you don't want me to have so much money, then stop giving it to me."

–Lysander

People kept on saying it. They kept on saying that the streak was soon to be over. That Bunny Computers was going to slow down, hit the wall like so many other companies that got too big too fast. A big company didn't run that way, they said. Bunny Computers was certainly becoming a big company, for sure.

But big companies were run by boards of people, not just a person or two. They were on the stock market, whereas Bunny Computers' money was locked up in banks. That is, if the company even had money, they said.

Bunny Computers was actually in debt. A debt exceeding millions of dollars. As soon as they got money, they spent it. Then they took out yet another loan, using whatever they had just bought as capital. Economic experts went over and over the money reports, which were available to the public to see. Almost everything that Bunny Computers did was open to the public eye, at least everything except Odd. After looking at the numbers over and over again, the experts agreed. The only way the company was going to be able to avoid bankruptcy is

if they tripled their income. When Drew heard that, he went pale and ran to make a phone call. He came back sweating and smiling, "Odd says he's going to quadruple it."

Which he did. The buildings went up, computer stores, wireless towers, even giant freighters and oil pumps. Drew actually got a break, as he had five experts in different areas now taking direct orders from Odd. Drew and the other five had three assistants each to help them keep up with what they had to do, and each of those assistants had an assistant. Drew's company had grown massive, and it was beginning to tell. Helaman Valley had grown swollen with factories and apartments for the workers flocking in. Forest went down and steel went up. Drew wondered what caused these people to abandon their old jobs, families, and homes. Some were unemployed before, so they made sense, but most weren't. It wasn't the money, they got paid the same wages as anyone else. When he mentioned this to Odd, all he got was a sardonic laugh and the comment, "Sheep, Mr. Howell. They're followers, and want to be in on the biggest thing since sliced bread, as the saying goes."

Drew wondered when Odd had heard that saying. He said, "Most people aren't sheep."

"Some are. *You* are." Odd said. Then he hung up.

Odd had been in a bad mood for a long time lately. Partly lack of sleep, but partly the fact that Drew was standing up for himself, which Odd hated. Drew now demanded no more than eight hours work per day, the reason for all the other assistants and helpers. He also declared a right to refuse Odd's directions. He hadn't used that yet, but it hung like a black cloud over every phone call. Another black cloud appeared when Drew said he could add more conditions later on. Odd had been furious, and even began shouting. That's when Drew had demanded respect from Odd, only escalating his temper. Then Drew had hung up. Odd had learned pretty quickly to respect Drew after that. Besides, Jess had actually been pleased with Drew, for the first time in a while.

Things were looking up.

That's what Drew was doing right now. He was looking up the giant sheet of glass that was his new fifty story skyscraper. Odd had wanted to build it in New York, but Drew refused, so here it was in his tiny little town, casting a black square over Main Street every evening. There should have been a million laws against that, but Drew's lawyers had sat down for a nice long talk with the city council, and the papers had been signed. So there it was.

To Drew, it felt wrong.

Of course, it was horrendous going to work there. There was construction on both the parking complex across the street to house all the cars, and the new highway. The town council had been frantic over all the new buildings, but was afraid to scare away all the new tax and growth opportunities. Now it was a scramble to build new roads, new public facilities. Every piece of land that was for sale was automatically purchased by one of Drew's assistants, no matter the cost.

Odd wanted it all. Now there were houses, grocery stores, and gas stations, all owned by Drew.

Drew realized what was going on.

It was an assembly line.

First, somebody would order a computer. The order would be processed in a building next to the factory that made the computer. The factory got a large portion of the needed materials from mines not too far away, built the computers, and packed it in a box from another assembly line, using tape from a company-owned supplier. The boxes were loaded on the company's delivery trucks, which used the company's gas to deliver them to their new owners along with a magazine with all the new latest accessories to make it all better, for a price. Even on the computer itself, it was all designed. All software, music, movies, everything could be bought from Bunny Computers, and since it was being bought on a company computer, there was a special discount so you would have no reason to go anywhere else.

Nothing was left out.

Of course, the other companies didn't go down without a fight. They couldn't reverse engineer the amazing computers, as hard as they tried, but they tried other things. None of it worked. Whenever they tried, Odd would pull out his greatest weapon: stubbornness.

It happened first with a gas station. A large gas company built a gas station right next to one of Drew's. Drew thought nothing of it, but began to notice something. The gas at Odd's station was always exactly ten cents cheaper. No matter the price on the other station, Odd's just so happened to be less that day. Then he noticed that when the competitor offered a large drink for $1.50, his station had the exact same size for $1.25. 2 for the price of 1 became 3 for the price of 1. Half off became two-thirds off. The other station began to lower its prices, but Drew's station was always just a little bit less.

It even went to the point that Drew knew they had to be losing money. He was about to say something, and had even pulled out his phone to call Odd when he saw it.

The other gas station was going out of business. Whoever owned that line of gas was leaving before they lost any more money. And like the ultimate insult, Drew's gas station now bore a gas price exactly ten cents higher.

It wasn't a new idea, of course. Simply out-compete the competition, and when they close up and leave, raise the prices to get all the money you had lost on the deal. But no one did it as fiercely as Odd. Drew was learning that even if it cost hundreds of thousands of dollars, Odd had to win. If he saw any kind of competition, it was crushed. Crushed just like what had used to be under the skyscraper. Drew knew there had been no other way. The only spot of available land in an area that they were allowed to build the skyscraper just so happened to be Drew's computer store. Or at least it *had* been his computer store. Now, ton upon ton of black, glimmering glass stabbed the sky.

A huge sign jutted out of the top of the tower, with the black shadow of a rabbit head and the word *BunnyWorks*. Not computers anymore, Drew reminded himself with a sort of happy sadness. Jess was happy, at least. He was standing up for himself, smiling a real smile on television instead of the grimace he had used to use. But Drew had the feeling something was wrong, like he was missing something. Or had missed it, and it was gone. He felt separated, like a passenger on a roller coaster he only partially controlled. Was this what it was like standing up for real? Drew had been waiting for this moment his whole life, a moment when he would actually be in charge of something big, something he could be proud of. It didn't matter that he didn't understand it all, that he didn't really care about gas or bottom lines or growth charts. It just mattered that he was finally calling the shots, that people listened a little bit instead of just walking right past. Drew even told himself that it was worth what he had lost. Just because he hadn't seen an animal in months meant nothing. Or at least, he didn't think it did.

Not like there was time for that now, he had to get to work. He walked towards the front doors, shiny shoes crackling as they stepped on something on the sidewalk. A single animal food pellet, now smeared as brown dust across the brand new sidewalk.

Drew looked down, and paused a second, considering the smear. Then he shrugged and walked on inside.

CHAPTER 29

"Imagine you went to sleep, and during the night everyone else stayed up. You get up, and you've missed it all, and you need to catch up quick. That's what hibernation is like."

–Arlen

"Mirada!" Arlen practically screamed as he dove out of the sky, "What's going on? When did it happen?" He seemed to trip in the air as he got closer, "Mirada? Is that y—"

Mirada jumped in shock, running a few feet as Arlen plowed face-first into the muddy ground. The snow was almost all melted, but today a thick brown slush coated everything. Spring was almost here, and that meant the bats were done hibernating. Mirada looked up to see some bats flying back to their caves, retreating from the dawn light. They squeaked fiercely, as if agitated.

"What? What's happening?"

"Down at the marshy place, where the river spreads out into that boggy stuff? Marshfly?" Arlen said, shaking himself to get the slush off. He adjusted the horribly dirty cloth over his eyes, "We were just there. We all saw. How on earth did it happen?"

"Marshfly...? I have no idea what you're talking about." Mirada said, squinting to see him. It was hard to see in the morning nowadays, for some reason. Her eyes got misty, like

there was dirt in them. Maybe there was.

"You haven't seen it?" Arlen said, his voice dropping a little, "None of the bunnies know?"

"Not any up here. We don't go down towards town to look for food, that's nuts!"

"No, there aren't any nuts." Arlen said, "Only bugs."

"I... sorry, Lysander said that to me. I don't actually know what it means."

"Okay...?" Arlen cocked his head, "But you have to come see."

Mirada frowned, "You mean now?"

"Now." Arlen took off, fluttering and squeaking until he landed on a tree branch some distance above Mirada, "Come on, I need to get home soon."

Mirada began to hop after him. He kept moving from branch to branch, leading her through the forest towards the base of the canyon. The place where the river split apart was somewhat close to the town. Mirada was fine at first, but the slush got in between her toes, soaking through her fur and freezing her skin. Worse, it was muddy. About halfway down, Mirada's legs began to ache. Then burn. Her stomach seemed to be eating itself, and not doing a very good job of it either. Her legs shook as the strength left them. Arlen didn't say anything, but she saw his normally placid face shift slowly into a frown. He moved between branches slower and slower, waiting for her to catch up.

Finally, Mirada heard it. A huge screech, like a hawk. She gasped, darting for cover, her weak legs slipping on the slush and landing her flat on her face. Mud streaked across her eyes, and she felt ready to cry. She probably looked hideous right now.

"Mirada, are you okay?" Arlen whispered in her ear, completely calm, "You don't sound so good. Are you sick?"

"H-hawk." Mirada whispered.

"That's not a hawk. That's the humans." Arlen said. A whole new form of terror gripped Mirada.

Humans! Machines! Adrenaline roared through her, filling her with all her remaining strength. It was almost enough to get up, but not quite. After struggling to move for a second, she gave up, lying in the freezing slush.

"Something is wrong with you." Arlen said, fluttering into the air. He flew around her, chirping erratically. Finally he landed, "The bunnies ran out of food, huh?"

Mirada said, "No."

Arlen was quiet. He sniffed, chirped and said, "But when I squeak, there's less of you. You used to be a lot, lot bigger. You're starved."

"I'm not starved. It's just that normally I'm fat. Now I'm not. That's what it is, okay? I'm thin, yes. Not starved." Mirada said, "Just because I don't gorge myself on every little bit of food…"

Arlen sighed, "I guess Lysander hasn't just been messing with humans. He's messed with you too."

Mirada didn't answer. Arlen sucked in a breath, "I'm sorry, that was cruel. I'm really sorry. Look… it's only ten more steps. Think you can do that, and then take a rest?"

"Yeah, alright." Mirada began to move forward slowly, legs shaking. She saw up ahead a cliff, her misty vision blurring the edge. She arrived at the edge, and rested her head on it, nose hanging just over. She sat for a few minutes as unusual sounds rose. Groans, screeches, clangs and shouting in human voices. Then she saw it.

The town had used to just sit there, like a distant puddle of small houses and low buildings. Now in the center of the city huge beasts of metal rose, things of grey and black that blocked off whole sections of the town. And below her, in what had used to be the riverbed at the edge of town, beasts raged. Humans swarmed everywhere beneath massive orange and yellow things, cars that were three times as big, with arms that shredded the trees and ground. A huge roll of shiny steel sparkled as it crushed the ground, pushed by a smoke-belching truck. Other trucks carried off entire hills of dirt. Another massive machine spat black liquid in a wide line. In horror, Mirada recognized the hardening liquid as the roads Lysander talked about.

Cars always stayed on roads, he said. Mirada had liked that, it made a certain area of safety, places where cars would stay, and not invade the other parts of the forest. Now she saw that these big cars, these servants of the humans, were making their own roads. And the entire forest was going to go down to give them room. The town was growing, teeming with more humans than Mirada had ever known existed.

Where had they all come from?

"This is Lysander's work." Arlen said, "He told me about this. That he could control the machines. This hasn't happened before, so it's him. Has to be."

"But we're safe, right?" Mirada said, "They won't keep this up for long, they won't get up to Waterlog and Darkdoor. This place was called Marshfly, right? It's not that important, bugs aren't important."

"Mirada, we bats eat bugs. This was where we got a whole lot of them." Arlen said, "Now there isn't a bug alive in the whole area. The humans are killing them and the place they live."

Mirada stared, thinking, "I'll ask Lysander. He'll know how to stop them, maybe even get your bugs back! He wouldn't just let you guys starve. I know he wouldn't."

"Starve? Like—" Arlen seemed about to say something, but stopped. After thinking, he said slowly, "Well, I guess you can ask, even though... never mind. Now you've seen. I just wanted you guys to know. It's not the bunny's problem, not yet, but... just so you guys know, you know? I have to get some sleep now, so you better head back. Lysander will probably want me to help him soon, so I need a rest." Arlen's voice seemed weary, like he hadn't slept a wink of his winter hibernation, "And we need to figure out the bug problem, too."

"I have to go... all the way up?" Mirada said, looking behind her. The climb down had been hard enough.

"Well, I can't stay all day while you take forever, the sun is coming out and I need sleep and... and... you look like you need a friend." Arlen sucked in his breath, "Okay... follow me."

Wearily, Arlen flew up to take his vigil on the first branch, holding back his weariness as Mirada began to slowly hop all the way back up.

CHAPTER 30

"We all react differently to fear. Some people get angry, or commanding, or even brave. Really, though, they are just as afraid as everyone else."

–Fallon

Drew stopped dead, hands frozen as he did up the last button on his suit. It was a beautiful day outside, the last of the snow melted off of his porch and leaving nothing but a few dark spots of wetness. Slowly, Drew came down the walkway, shoes splashing a little in the puddles left by receding snow.

"It's a federal offense to steal someone's mail, you know." He told the man who so casually leaned up to his mailbox, squinting and smiling cheekily at the morning sun. Cory Yalk smiled a big fake grin as he shuffled through Drew's mail. His gelled hair gleamed in the light.

Cory stood up straight, turning to Drew and smiling wider, "Wondered how long it was going to take you to get out here. You sleep late."

"I get up at six. I just do some things in the morning. Now give me my mail."

"Here, I'm not interested in those." Cory Yalk held out the letters. Drew grabbed them, but as he pulled away he noticed one envelope was still clutched in Cory's fingers. Cory pulled the letter back, and Drew coldly realized it was already open.

"Court summons." Cory said nonchalantly, pulling out the paper, "Mr. Drew Howell, blah, blah, blah, person is suing you, blah, blah, blah."

"How dare you!" Drew said in fury, grabbing the letter furiously, "Coming to my house and—"

"I'm not suing you!" Cory said, holding up his hands, "Read what it says."

Drew unfolded the letter, scanning it. As he did, he grew even more angry, Jess's strength giving him the energy to fight instead of back down, "These are ridiculous!"

"Of course they are." Cory said, folding his arms, "Use your brains, I know you have them somewhere."

"I don't understand." Drew said, "Why would anyone do this?"

Cory sighed, beginning to pace around Drew. Drew turned in confusion, trying to keep his eye on the sly reporter. He was so laid back, not like the others, always pestering for information. But he somehow got it anyway.

Cory stopped and said, "It's a grudge match. It's a war of information, and you know something they don't. Let me be plain. They know who you are, and that you own the company. But Odd is the one who made it all. They don't know anything about him. He might not even exist."

"I don't—"

"I know you don't have any idea!" Cory cut across, "I can see that. But they think you know Odd, who he is, what he wants. Somewhere, they still suspect you're him."

"What does that have to do with this?" Drew held up the letter.

"When you're in court, they have lawyers ask questions.

They can pay these lawyers to do whatever they want, it doesn't matter if they win or lose. They will ask questions, though. Lots of them. Investigate. Probably not about anything in that letter. They'll ask about Odd, for sure. You have to answer, especially since you're under oath. Unless you lied…" Cory's voice trailed off, and he raised an eyebrow like he was asking a question.

Drew frowned deeper. He wouldn't lie, of course not. He'd hate himself for it, and so would Jess. Not to mention the fact that everything he did was plastered on the news an hour after he did it. But he couldn't tell them what he didn't know. What if they thought he was lying anyway?

"Mr. Howell, I came to give you a warning. Maybe you will listen. Maybe not. The thing is that you have no idea what is happening. I don't. Odd is the one pulling all our strings."

"Not you." Drew said, "I saw you pull his strings, at that press conference. He hung up so he wouldn't have to answer your question."

"He called me."

Drew shot a look, "Odd did?" Cory didn't answer.

Drew moved over to Cory, resting his hand on his shoulder, "What did he act like? He acts different to different people, I've noticed."

"At first, demanding. I argued, and he became… withdrawn. Secluded, even." Cory blinked, his eyes unfocused, "That thing terrifies me."

"Thing."

"Surely you don't think he's human?" Cory said, looking up at Drew, "He doesn't act like that. He acts different."

"I don't know what to think. But he has to be human. Maybe a group of people?"

Cory shook his head, "Too much of an opinion. Too strong-willed, too quick for a group."

Drew said, "So what do you think?"

"I think he is terrifying. Maybe not human. Of course, he must look like a human, but it's obvious he isn't one. A human isn't like him. If he was born as one, he isn't anymore." Cory took a few steps away, staring at the grass. He scuffed his shoe in it a few times, "Mr. Howell, I can only warn you. You need to stop this."

"Why?"

"He is planning something. I don't know what, but I know that it will be horrible. Very bad."

"How do you know?"

Cory shook his head, walking down the street, "Odd wants revenge. I don't want to know what that means."

Drew watched, tapping the letter against his lips as Cory Yalk made his way slowly towards downtown.

CHAPTER 31

"The hardest choices to make are the ones you can't control."

–Fallon

Fallon circled, screeching repeatedly as he flew low over the ground. Nothing. A few flashes, here and there. That was the bugs, of course. Tiny dots of movement, irregular against the mass of leaves that made up the trees. But there were only a few, not near enough. Fallon wished again he still could go to Marshfly. That had been a mass of movement, bugs so thick that you just had to open your mouth to get a meal. You didn't have to chase them, or aim, because there were simply so many. Not now, though. Lysander had ruined that. He was ruining everything. Humans were invading, cars were making new roads, and everything he had worked to build was falling apart. He didn't know how or why, but he knew it had all started when Lysander came. It was far too obvious what had caused this.

His command was falling apart. Clan members were questioning him again. Even his closest circle, the group of bats he used to control the rest, were beginning to usurp his authority. What, they asked, made him in charge anyway? They did all the work. Fallon tried to explain that making decisions and giving orders was just as hard, but nobody believed him. He wasn't used to this. It reminded him of before he had risen to power, when the bats were just a mob, ruled by one tough guy who beat up the last. But under him, there was order. That was good, no matter what Arlen said.

That was being lost day by day. Especially now, with the food shortage. Without many large batches, Fallon had been forced to break up the bats into groups, send them off to different parts of the mountain to find a meal. But there was little water this year, which meant fewer bugs. Even the groups were beginning to split up, against his orders. Lone bats flew off, searching for food that wasn't there.

This is what happened without leadership. Anarchy, confusion. Fallon had to find a good food source soon, or anything could happen. So he kept searching, chirping softly, so softly his own ears could barely register it.

That is, until a sound came so loud and so close it deafened him instantly. Fallon screeched, flipping in the air, but cords of fleshy iron clamped around his chest, pinning a wing down and leaving the other uselessly flapping. Fallon felt himself drop fast, plummeting towards the ground. Chirping, he got the dim outline of feathers. Feathers?

Then he hit the ground. Whatever held him used him as cushioning, and he felt the bones in his body creak and groan under the pressure. There was a sharp snap as his wing twisted into an entirely new angle.

"Fallon." A voice croaked above him, throaty and high, like rasping metal on cars.

"Who are you?" Fallon croaked, his voice cracking and groaning under the pain that felt like a fire under him. It didn't go in waves or anything like that, it was just simple, constant

pain.

"You are Fallon." The voice said. Fallon blinked, but all he could see was a huge shape, some kind of monster. Fallon chirped, and saw the outline of a hawk. He whimpered.

The hawk suddenly squawked, letting go of Fallon and flapping frantically. It seemed to fall over, and struggled a moment before getting back on its feet. Fallon kept chirping, and finally saw why. One leg was fine, probably the one that had snagged him. The other was twisted, swollen.

"I caught bat." The hawk said, not moving from its spot but putting quite a bit of weight on its good leg, "Told about you, say you leader. So I find."

"Are you going to kill me?" Fallon asked. His voice was oddly steady, opposite to his heart and swimming head.

"Already eat two mouse. And bat." The hawk screeched softly, pulling up its leg for a fraction, then putting it down again. It bent oddly, "You remember? Your orders."

"Orders?"

The hawk limped over to Fallon, who still lay on the ground, nursing his wing, "I hunting, see bat. Chase bat. Bat not try to escape, fly straight, then go in tree. I about to go after, but see rabbit."

"Oh!" Fallon's mind connected the hawk to the attack on Lysander. But what had happened to its leg?

"Bunnies easier than bats. I think so. So I try to eat bunny. Then it bite me. You made trap!"

"It wasn't a trap." Fallon said, "I wanted you to eat him. I wanted him dead."

"I want dead too." The hawk said, it's voice guttural, pain driving it's rage. It scratched out another sentence, "But not me. Now your job."

"My…?" Fallon trailed off.

"Kill bunny." The hawk's blunt statement was like a knife through the night air.

Fallon gulped several times to maintain his composure as he processed the statement, "Why would I even try that? That's insane."

"I watch, want to find tricky bat. Now I do. As I look, see cave. Above waterfall, full bats."

Fallon gasped, flipping over so he wouldn't be facing the horrible hawk, "You know where Darkdoor is."

"You do what I say. You say no, I kill bats. All bats!"

"We could find a different cave. Run away." Fallon tried.

"No other cave. I know." The hawk let out a screech, and Fallon cringed. The hawk was right. Darkdoor was the only cave on the entire mountain. And even a few days in the open would prove deadly for a bat.

"If I kill him, you'll leave us alone?" Fallon said. He was desperately thinking for a way out. So much for his leadership. So much for having power over it all. It was so easy to give orders when you knew they would be followed. Now he had that end of the stick, and it was an awful feeling.

"No! You kill rabbit, I eat him. Then I stay away from cave. Still eat bats, but not go in cave." The hawk said, before its leg gave out again. It screeched in fury, and finally got into a sitting position, "And one thing too. I eat you."

"Eat…" Fallon couldn't finish.

"After you kill rabbit, I eat you. You tricked me, I kill." The hawk said, "But not go near cave. You say yes?"

"Never!" Fallon used his good wing to push him over to look at the hawk. His eyes were practically useless, but he narrowed them in defiance.

"I kill all bats." The hawk said, and began to flap, rising into the air.

"No! I'll do it!" Fallon said, "Please, leave them alone." He had to protect the clan. Arlen may not have agreed with Fallon before. He probably never would, and that hurt. But Fallon knew that without him, it was going to be chaos. Like it was right now.

The hawk hovered, turning towards him, "You have three suns." It left, screeching a night-shattering shout.

Fallon groaned, and sat up. He got almost six inches off the ground before his broken wing sent him crashing down again.

CHAPTER 32

"You have to know how to follow before you can lead."

—Fallon

"Mirada!" Darshep called as she was entering the cave. Mirada turned, shaking her head and trying to make her eyes adjust to the sudden change in light. Darshep stood just inside, Tysell standing by him. She was still scratchy looking, but almost free of muck. Her thin, hard body only had a small layer of dust, and her eyes sparkled with a vibrant brightness. But she wasn't smiling. That was what Mirada noticed most of all. Usually when Tysell and Darshep were by each other they would be smiling happily. Not now.

Mirada sneezed, and asked, "What?"

"Have you noticed there haven't been any predators around the caves for a long time?" Darshep asked.

Mirada frowned. There hadn't been predators near at all this summer, "I suppose. Maybe they're hunting elsewhere."

"No, they aren't." Darshep said.

Tysell added, "They ain't here, but they're all over around us. They just don't come near our caves."

Darshep nodded, practically dripping authority. Mirada couldn't ever remember him cowering. He said, "It's that Ly-

sander freak. First he scared the fur off that fox and then bit that hawk."

"That was last fall." Mirada said, "You think predators stay away that long? Besides, isn't this a good thing?"

Darshep frowned, turning to the side. A group of bunnies sat in another tunnel, staring with wide eyes, "Take the other tunnel."

They left in a hurry. Darshep twisted his head, as if getting ready to fight, and took a few steps towards Mirada. She stepped back, looking away from his eyes. He sniffed, and scowled, noticing her appearance. But at least she was thin, it didn't matter if she had bad breath. It was getting too hard to walk down to the river every day to wash herself, and she had to conserve all her energy to find a little bit of food. Not much, of course, but enough that she could lose weight and still eat. She'd adjust eventually, she was sure of it. Then Lysander would notice her.

Darshep said, "There is only one thing a predator is afraid of, and that's humans. The fact that they are afraid of Lysander proves one thing."

Mirada laughed, but had to stop herself as it began to develop into a cough, "Don't be stupid, he's a bunny!"

"That bunny hurts everything he's around! Just look at what he's done to you." Darshep said. Mirada cringed, but Darshep continued, "I treat Tysell with the utmost respect and honor. It's obvious from looking at you that Lysander doesn't."

"He just needs to notice..." Mirada trailed off.

Tysell stepped forward, resting her head on Darshep's thick fur, "She thinks she's fat, Darshy. Ain't nothing but fur, but she wants to look pretty for that nut."

Darshep closed his eyes and took a steadying breath,

"Look, Mirada, I can respect that, I guess. If you want to chase after that creep and hurt yourself in the process I can't stop you, as much as I wish I could. We sure are missing you on the food-finding, though it doesn't look like you're so good at that anymore."

"What do you want?"

"The bats from Darkdoor sent us a messenger. They're planning… an unfortunate event for Lysander. They refuse any negotiation."

Mirada's eyes widened as she figured it out, "How on Earth? Why would they do that?"

"I don't know. Neither did the messenger. These are direct orders from their leader."

"And all the bats plan to follow him?"

Darshep grimaced, "It isn't like here, Mirada. Here you can steal from the food stores all day long, and I can't stop you." Mirada cringed as she realized Darshep must have known all along, but he just kept going, "With the bats, though, they aren't like that. The leader of the bats, Fallon, has complete control. If he gives an order, a bat is expected to follow, even if that bat doesn't agree. So it doesn't matter what most of the bats think, it just matters that it's going to happen."

"What are they going to do to him?"

Darshep hung his head, "I'm very sorry, Mirada."

Mirada shook, her heart pounding, "No."

Tysell whispered to Mirada, her eyes sad and tear-filled, "That's why we gotta tell you, Mirada. You visit him. If you're there when they come, who knows what'll happen?"

"I'll tell you what'll happen." Mirada said, sneezing furiously and coughing, "We'll send them packing. Bats are tiny compared to any bunny."

"You're in no condition to fight." Darshep said, "And you aren't a predator or even male. You have no idea how to defend yourself. No bunny does."

"Bats aren't fighters either. So if you don't mind," Mirada snorted heavily, "I have a job to do."

Mirada hopped, limping, out of the cave, stopping at the entrance and having a coughing fit before finally moving on. Darshep sniffed quietly, watching her leave as Tysell huddled nearer to him. He looked at her and noticed her huge, worried eyes, and sniffed again.

"Well, I guess that settles it." Darshep said. He sighed, looking away from Tysell. She tried to move to look at his face, but he just shuffled out of her way. He drew himself up straight, hoping the posture would give him courage.

"Darshep, it ain't your fault—"

"I'm not blaming myself, that isn't the problem. The problem is that I'm in charge, a little bit. I have to set an example."

"What?"

"I should just hide, or run. That would make sense..." Darshep said, "But now it looks like that's not going to be an option."

"Darshep, the bats are crazy!" Tysell said, huddling against him, "They got a hawk last time."

"Then I'll just have to hope they don't try it again." Darshep said, shrugging her off. He turned towards her, "Tysell, if I didn't do this, I wouldn't... I wouldn't be as brave as you want, as strong."

Tysell bit her lip. Darshep sighed, then leaned in and softly rubbed his nose against hers, "I'll be back soon." Then he turned, and with a single backwards glance, hopped out into the sunshine.

CHAPTER 33

"I think every kid should get a coupon at birth for a one day vacation from life. I know I need it."

–Drew Howell

"Okay!" Drew announced as he marched into his office, "Everyone out!"

A dozen faces turned to him, their babble dying on the air. His experts and assistants sat at a long table in the conference room that led to his office.

He stared at them, "Well?"

Slowly, still staring, they got up, gathering their things and exiting, mumbling to each other remarks probably about Drew. Papers were shuffled, whispering like a sour wind. Drew scowled, heading to his office door. He opened it and got on the other side, shutting it softly behind him.

Then he collapsed against it and slid slowly down to the floor. He stared at his desk in front of him, blocking out the window. He had been at the courts all day. All week, in fact, going to several different courts for many different trials for a plethora of crimes which he hadn't committed. It was indeed a ploy to get information, a ploy to ask him questions while he was required to sit in a chair and answer them. After the first time, everyone else had caught on and joined in on the fun.

Even Odd was at him, angry that so much money was being spent on lawyers.

Drew didn't know how to stop it. The only person happy with him was his wife. That made it bearable. Jess even said that they couldn't sue him for the same crime more than once, something that Drew felt a little comforted by. A little. His entire staff was hating his absence, since they had trouble doing anything without his supreme authority behind the orders. Ordering them out was probably not his best move.

Drew dialed Odd's number. As he rang, he organized his thoughts. He was actually the only one who could still call Odd. The only people that knew Odd's phone number were him and the cell phone company, who had it as a private number and so couldn't give it out. Literally couldn't. A spy in the cell phone company had even tried. It had been all over the news. The spy had taken the encrypted files of cell phone numbers home, where he attempted to decipher them on his computer. His computer crashed, and the power grid in his town instantly failed. When they rebooted, every computer started up with the *BunnyWorks* logo, something which still hadn't been fixed.

There were also numerous tales of hackers who tried to log into the *BunnyWorks* network. One's computer turned on its disk drive so fast the CD exploded, denting the computer's metal frame. Another computer was reportedly shifting through every color of the rainbow. A third was said to laugh maniacally every time you tried to click the mouse.

BunnyWorks claimed that the happenings were entirely out of their control, caused by some kind of interference not designed to be on their firewall. They were trying to fix the problem, they said. Drew knew they were, but he also knew the message was obvious to everyone.

No one messed with Odd.

What really worried Drew was the increased stories of other problems. Computers by other companies slowed down to the speed of cold tar, or broke for no reason. *BunnyWorks* computers worked fine, and he had a feeling they would continue to work as long as Odd called the shots.

"Hello Drew." Odd said when he picked up the phone, "Are you planning to get to work anytime soon?"

"Actually, it's close to five, so I'm going home in a few minutes." Drew said. Odd was silent. Drew continued, "Look, I can't keep this up. I need a little help from you."

"A little help? Haven't I been working, slaving to—"

"That's your problem!" Drew cut across, "We both know that all this is your thing, I'm the one that's the helper. Your little slave."

"What do you want?" Odd asked, his voice scratching. It almost sounded like he had a cold or something.

"I want you to stop this."

"The company?"

"No, I'm not stupid. I mean my suffering." Drew said, "Look, I may not be as smart as you, I know that. But I know some things. I know that a few seconds in front of a camera for you can end months of my suffering. I know that a happy person works harder, so if I was happier I would get more done for you, especially since I wouldn't be in court all day long. I also know that you can't possibly stay secret forever. It's impossible."

"I've been invisible this long." Odd said. Drew stood up, walking across the room and sitting in his desk. It was time to get serious, pull out his bravery for the next few steps.

"Can we just meet in person?" Drew offered, "Talk face to face? If only I could see you, know you were real—"

"You *have* seen me." Odd said.

"What?"

"We used to know each other, quite well." Odd said, "The last time we saw each other was the night of that storm."

"I didn't see anybody that night... I was checking on my store."

"You saw me. You just don't remember." Odd said, "We aren't discussing this any longer."

Drew readjusted the phone to make sure Odd wouldn't miss a word, "You, my friend, are the biggest thing on the internet and the news and the world. You are in the spotlight already, it's just that you manage to still cover your face. It's not going to hurt to have a picture taken, no matter how many mirrors you've broken."

"It can't be done." Odd said, and coughed, "It's impossible."

"Look, I know you try to get me to do things by putting pressure on me. That's how you do everything. So if it always works for you, then it should work once for me."

Odd was silent, but Drew knew he had heard. He continued, "Which is why I have booked the auditorium in this skyscraper for a public speech in your name. I have also arranged for it to be recorded and globally televised. The event is in four days, at exactly 7 p.m. The entire world will expect your presence."

"I won't do it." Odd said, his tone one of punishment-laced warning.

"What happens if you don't? People will refuse to trust you, or me. They'll stop buying, send us angry letters. This will put a dent in your plan the size of your big fat brain, Odd." Drew retaliated with an insult not unlike one of Odd's, "You have no choice."

"I refuse." Odd said, though his voice cracked, and he coughed several times, "I didn't think you would ever try to betray me like this. When this is over, Drew, you will pay like the rest of them."

"I just want a break, Odd." Drew said, before flipping the phone shut so hard he was surprised it didn't snap. Then he gave up, and numbly broke it in half himself. He tossed it in the wastebasket, thinking sardonically that he could probably get a *Bunny Works* phone for free.

Then, his eyes widened, "The rest of them?"

CHAPTER 34

"It's awesome how brute force smashes everything in its path. Plain, simple, effective. Cool, really."

–Zach Erikson

The bats of Darkdoor cave screamed, chirping and squeaking, flapping in terror. It was a black whirlwind, a cloud of confusion that streamed out the doorway into the sunlight. Arlen woke with them, panicking. He was buffeted, knocked from his perch by wingtips rushing past. He tried to right himself, but couldn't in the confusion. Rushing shapes were everywhere, his squeaking lost amidst the chorus of others. He couldn't hear anything, blind as the chorus of chirps flashed in his brain, the images all confusing together. Bats could time chirps and use each others' so that didn't happen, but in a panic, it wasn't going to work.

Then he did hear something. A hawk's scream. The screech froze his blood, his wings locking in place and sending him into a faster freefall. He hit several bodies, and then the ground.

"Fallon." He whispered, "Fallon, where are you?"

He waited, waited until the bats had all left, scattering to the winds. The hawk didn't chase, in fact it hadn't caught a single bat. Instead, it flew slowly deeper in, taking it's time. Its eyes probably weren't used to such darkness. Then it landed, and chirping a little, Arlen saw it stood over Fallon. His stomach turned. Fallon couldn't fly, not with his broken wing. Arlen watched, unable to move but terrified to see his brother die.

"You say yes to what I say. I say three sun, and you do it. This third sun!" The bird said, following by a screech so loud Fallon rolled over, grunting in pain as his injured wing moved.

"I'm sorry, it's just that a bat doesn't really have any weapons—"

"You promise!" The hawk let out a screech so loud that Arlen cringed. The echo along the cave walls amplified the noise, making it ten times louder, lasting twice as long. It was the sound of death, a cruel, painful death. Fallon wasn't dead, though, and it looked like the hawk didn't plan to kill him.

"Look, I'll get that bunny for you... but you have to help." Fallon whispered.

"No! YOU KILL!" The bird screamed, flapping its wings and hopping on one leg. Arlen then saw the other, and it clicked together in his mind. This wasn't good.

"We have a plan!" Fallon said, raising one wing as if pleading. He had to talk lying on his back, at complete mercy of everything. Fallon said, "Look to your right."

The hawk did, and jumped back, "Porcupine!"

"Just a few quills. And they were not easy to get, believe me." Fallon said.

Arlen silently agreed. Fallon had actually ordered them to harass a porcupine, which could have killed some of them if they weren't careful. They had to be close enough and annoying enough to be a real nuisance, but not close enough that the thing could touch them. Eventually, they got it so annoyed and desperate that it begged them to go away. After they convinced it to scrape against a tree and get some of its quills off, they let it

go. Carrying the quills back to the cave had proved even more dangerous, and one bat was even stabbed. It took until morning to get the quill out, and the bat still wasn't feeling so good.

"We'll attack him with these… But that won't kill him. You'll have to finish him off when we drag him out of the cave."

"I not eat rabbit with porcupine! I eat quill? No!"

"Well, I don't know any other way! I'm not a predator; I don't have claws or anything!"

"You have many bats."

"None of which can take on a bunny! Those things are three times the size of us! And they have *claws!* I would lose too many."

"Then how?" Hawk said, "How kill?"

Fallon raised his head, "I had a plan, but you said no to it. Now you get a plan."

The hawk screeched in fury, flapping a short distance away. It scraped at the layer of grime on the cave floor with its weak leg. At least, that's what Arlen was gathering from what he heard. His hearing picked up every minute sound, his brain putting it together like a giant jigsaw puzzle. His lungs seemed to flood with cold in each breath, fear adding to the freezing effect and making him shiver. The cave was far too cold, the cold night of the unusually cold spring driving every speck of heat from his body. He couldn't see, couldn't squeak because that would tell the hawk where he was. That would be a bad idea, almost as bad as Fallon's.

It was, frankly, a horrible plan. Worse was the fact he actually planned to kill something. Worst was the fact that a hawk was forcing him to do it. But why was he listening? Was he sacrificing the life of everyone just so he didn't have to die? Arlen shook his head. Fallon wouldn't do something like that.

He couldn't.

The hawk screeched, turning, "I think plan!" It sounded almost happy, "You attack bunny, get bunny out cave. That all you do."

"Then you kill him?"

"No. Bring friend. Attack at sun time."

Fallon raised his head, but the hawk was already starting to fly away. Fallon called after it, "You have a friend? Another hawk?"

"No." The hawk said as it exited the cave, "Raccoon."

Fallon's head had been lifted, staring blearily after the hawk. His glazed-over eyes squeezed shut in agony, and his head flopped onto the soft cave floor like a dead fish. Weakly, he whispered, "We are *so* dead."

Arlen completely agreed.

CHAPTER 35

"I kill all! Brain smart, claw stupid. Claw kill brain. Brain no kill. I kill!"

–Hawk

Just a few more lines of code. That's all it needed. A few more typed words, maybe two hundred, or fewer. Then it was done. Lysander narrowed his eyes, grinning. They would see. Drew would see. They would see that you didn't force Odd to show himself, you don't mess with him. He'll mess with you.

They all deserved it, of course. Lysander's head ached, a combination of his not-entirely-healed claw wounds, his lack of sleep, and the black burn across one ear. It was getting worse. It might even kill him. For now, though, he was alive. He was in pain, both day and night in pain since that horrible moment, that human death trap and that storm. Normally he could ignore it, act natural so every bunny thought he was at least a little normal. Of course, Lysander knew he wasn't normal in the slightest. He was different, he was special. He was gifted with the power to beat the humans at their own game. It was so ironic. A human machine had given one of the weakest animals imaginable the power to understand, listen to the language of machines and figure out how they worked. Lysander could feel the computer under his paws almost like a living thing. It breathed numbers in and out, pumping strings of code through tiny vessels, slamming it through the heart, the CPU, and spitting it into every other part of the computer. Under Lysander's paws, it was learning a final trick, the last string of numbers and letters and commands it would ever execute.

It had taken a while. Too long. In fact, Lysander had it practically done since before he had contacted Drew. But he hadn't ever finished it. He had to wait, had to let his business grow, his presence be brought into everyone's homes, their businesses. He had expected it to happen quicker, but that hadn't been the case. It was ready now, though. He had a link to every electric device connected to the internet or any wireless communication. Some of it had even been easier than expected. Lysander had thought it would be hard to infiltrate governments, especially military. But they had bought his computers, wanting to be the best in the world, ahead of the other countries. He had gotten in there without even trying.

Now he just had to finish. Lysander shook his head, fighting the burning flash of pain that kept coming back. The old wounds ached. If only he could concentrate. If only Mirada would leave his front door and that busy Darshep would stop digging next door. He didn't believe those bats were going to come, not even with the shivering Arlen who stood right behind him.

"Lysander—"

"Quiet." Lysander ordered. He had begun to ignore Arlen the instant he had tried to tell his story. Something about a hawk and a raccoon and Fallon. None of it mattered. All that mattered was these last few lines. Done. Finished. All that was needed now was a quick read-through for any bugs. Lysander chuckled at this, laughing at the idea he would ever make a mistake, but began to scroll through anyway.

Just a few more minutes.

The attack came out of nowhere. All that Mirada saw were glimmers, as if the stars were flickering, turning off like the lights in the city. But it was bats. They charged down, swarming in a massive rustling cloud. Mirada spread her shaky legs for balance, standing at the edge of the cave mouth to fight them off as best she could.

Nothing happened. Mirada shook her head, and realized with a shock the bats weren't attacking her. The massive cloud flew straight into Darshep's hole. He had been digging one next to Lysander's, to give him a place to live as he watched for the bats. Now he was the one getting attacked.

Mirada stared, confused, until it clicked. They had seen her at the front of Lysander's cave, and assumed it was her hole. Therefore, the other one had to be Lysander's. Mirada shouted, fear streaming through her shaking body, "Darshep!"

There was a shout, the sound of scuffling. Mirada tried to move forward, charge to the rescue. A cloud of black battered her back, and she cried out, squinting. She realized she really should have eaten that day. Like always, she had been thinking of how fat she probably looked. Now, her legs shook and her stomach moaned, begging for more food at the worst time, and sapping her strength when she wanted it most.

Darshep shouted twice, and there was a thudding sound. Arlen materialized next to Mirada, "They're trying to drag him out. They must think he's Lysander."

"He has black fur." Mirada said, the fact something to grab onto in the chaos she could only watch, "Lysander's is white."

"They don't know that. Not easy for a bat to see colors in the dark."

"Tell them to be quiet." Lysander said, coming out behind them, "I can't concentrate with this noise."

Mirada and Arlen turned, faces blank. Arlen took a few flaps forward, landing right in front of Lysander. The bat cloud screeched and roiled, buffeting them. But the swarm hadn't seemed to even notice any of them, intent on cramming into the cave, mindless to the other bunnies so nearby.

"Something's wrong with you, really wrong." Arlen said, his voice soft, "You really have no idea what's going on, do you? You don't see."

"See what?"

"It's too late, anyway." Arlen turned, looking away. Mirada stared, biting her lip and hoping. Surely Lysander would do something. He would stop the bats, make sure Darshep wasn't hurt. They'd all be safe.

Darshep screamed.

Mirada turned to see the bats retreating together. They were flapping hard and dragging Darshep behind them. His black fur gleamed in the moonlight, shining and taut from the many little feet that gripped it. One of his eyelids was cut, soaking an area of fur around it with dark liquid. He growled, tried to pull himself back into the cave against the bats. There were so many that they hauled him against his will, his claws plowing tiny scratches in the ground but stopping nothing.

"No!" There was a voice above. Mirada, Arlen, and Lysander looked up to see Fallon. A group of five bats were hauling him along, obviously straining with the weight, mostly gripping his fur with their feet. Fallon's broken wing hung limply. Fallon shouted, "That isn't Lysander. He's the white one!"

The bats stopped, letting go of Darshep. They seemed to pause in the air, looking between Mirada and Lysander.

"The shiny one." Fallon added in exasperation.

The bats flew for Lysander. He tried to bolt for his hole, but it was too late. The bats seized every visible piece of fur, dragging him across to the middle of the field. Then they stopped, holding him there. Mirada took a step forward, but twenty bats landed in front of her, blocking her path. Higher on the hill, a line of bunnies was forming. They watched silently. They had crowded into huddles. Staring outwards, it was obvious that the only thing they cared about was their own safety, but kept an eye on the fight so they could know if they needed to hide. Mirada remembered when she had been like that. It had been before Lysander had come. Now, she was changed for good or bad, and it didn't really matter which.

Fallon was brought down to the ground, set gently on the grass. In his good wing tip, his claws curled around a porcupine quill. He said softly, "So here we are."

Lysander glared at him under the crushing weight of the mob on top of him. They had stopped flying, but were stacked two deep in some places, making sure he wouldn't try to get up. He still struggled, every heave of his body sending one or two bats cascading off the pile in an undignified heap. They just climbed back on. He kept fighting until one rather large push sent him down so hard it knocked his breath out. He grunted, wincing as he felt his ribs bend and almost break under the pressure. Through the film of red that covered his eyes, he saw the dim outlines of Mirada, Darshep, and Arlen. Why hadn't they run? He just couldn't understand why. All he could understand was pain, and the odd lack of fear. All he felt was anger.

"You should know, I didn't mean to ever kill you." Fal-

lon said, "I told Arlen I would, but that's because I wanted to spread that. I knew he would tell. I wanted to change you. But that didn't work. You're messing with the order, Lysander. Things aren't the same anymore."

"Maybe that's a good thing." Lysander said, and grunted as he tried to draw breath. He twisted his head in frustration, knocking off three bats

"Change isn't a good thing. We were surviving. You change things and we might die."

"You might have an easier life."

Fallon laughed, "Nothing's easy for a bat, friend. You're a bunny, right down there with us, so you know. Predators own our lives. All we can do is run and hide. And sometimes even that doesn't work. See me? I thought I was good at avoiding the big bad guys, but then… a hawk got me. Same one that almost got you." Fallon managed to shift his broken wing, closing his eyes and frowning as he did it.

"But you escaped."

"Did I?" Fallon said. He closed his eyes, listening. There was nothing.

Then, a bush behind Fallon exploded in a shower of leaves. A massive grey beast thundered down on the ground right behind Fallon. The thing loped forward, an uneven gait making it roll like an ocean wave. It went straight over Fallon, who squeaked just before he disappeared under the bulk. In the moonlight flashed large black eyes, framed by a black and white mask. A smell, dark and sickly, waved in the air in front of the creature. Even that smell was terrifying.

The bats scattered.

Mirada ran forward, but Darshep was ahead of her. He ran out in front, standing directly before the raccoon. He

roared, "Stop!"

The raccoon glared, "Stoopig bunglies, arrgh…" It swayed a little. It shook its head, like it was trying to rid itself of flies, but there wasn't a single bug in the cold spring night. The raccoon stopped shaking as Darshep addressed it again, his paws spread wide to look big. The raccoon watched as though it was half-asleep.

"You don't want to do this. I know you're probably hungry, but this is insane." Darshep said, "Why attack animals when others already caught them for you? There's no honor in that. Kill me if you have to, but leave them alone."

Arlen whispered, "Mirada, look at that raccoon."

Mirada looked, wondering what was up. Why hadn't it attacked? What was going on? It was breathing heavy, an oddly thin chest heaving back and forth. It was also leaning to the side, off balance.

Mirada recognized it instantly. Softly, she whispered, her voice splintering, "Rabies."

Darshep turned, eyes widening at the mention of the horrible word, "What?"

The raccoon charged, but fell, crashing to the ground for no reason. It snarled, spitting thick saliva as it attempted to crawl to its feet. Lysander took a few steps back, his eyes widening. Darshep barely held his ground, yelling back, "Run!"

The raccoon pounced, going straight over Darshep and aiming for Lysander. Lysander rolled out of the way. Arlen took for the air. The raccoon curled up and crashed, dirt flying as it slid to the doorway of Lysander's cave. Its tail draped across the entrance to Darshep's cave. Mirada looked up for the other bunny caves, but couldn't see them in the dark. The watching bunnies were gone.

"Gragl! Stlupig bunglies!" The raccoon roared, growling low in its throat. A spout of syrupy slime slid out of its mouth as it had a coughing fit. Its breath seemed to pervade the air in a thick cloud of steam. Mirada nearly gagged from the smell, even though she was far away. Slowly, the raccoon got up. Then it was off, a silver flash going straight for Darshep. He yelped and took off, moving towards Lysander. The raccoon was far slower than Darshep, in fact any bunny. There was no chance he would be caught.

Then the raccoon suddenly switched, jumping for Lysander, jaws open. He merely stared, face blank, no one home.

"No!" Mirada shouted. But Darshep had turned, and actually ran for the raccoon. The raccoon attempted to jump over him, but its legs failed, the rabies causing them to tangle. He fell, going straight over Darshep like a car hitting a deer.

Lysander's instincts finally kicked in, and he began to run. The raccoon turned to give chase, but stopped, clawing at the air. Arlen was dive-bombing him, yelling. Arlen turned, hovering, "Get out of here, guys!"

The raccoon swiped, taking advantage of Arlen's distraction. Arlen grunted as the claw hit him through the air, down towards the river. He squeaked once before smacking into the ground. The raccoon turned. Lysander was running towards his cave, Mirada standing just next to the mouth of it. The raccoon charged, quickly outstripping the slow Lysander.

Mirada could only watch in horror.

He should have easily gotten away. But he couldn't. She hadn't ever seen Lysander run fast, and apparently even his life being on the line wasn't enough to make him even worry about speed. He wasn't going to make it.

"Gill bunglies!" The raccoon screamed; spit flying

from its open mouth. Its paws shredded the ground, the sound grinding. Mirada couldn't take it. She jumped forward, stepping just between Lysander and the raccoon without making a sound. She closed her eyes in the split second before it hit her.

CHAPTER 36

"I once asked someone how they were, and they said bad… Then I realized I had no answer for that. I expected them to say they were fine. I guess I expect people to say fine."

–Drew Howell

Lysander only registered what happened a split second after he made it inside the cave. He turned just in time to see the raccoon twist its head around, angry, before flipping the limp body of Mirada a yard into the air. Her body hit the ground softly, her thin, twisted frame barely pushing down the grass at all, light as air.

The raccoon turned, walking slowly towards the cave. Its chest heaved, and it gasped for air, tipping first one way, then the other. It was almost at the mouth of the cave, its own mouth foaming, when something happened.

It tipped, and kept tipping, slamming to the ground. Its body seemed to melt across the grass like slushy snow, and a trail of spittle hung across the grass stalks. The raccoon wheezed like a broken car.

It convulsed rapidly, body seizing again and again. Lysander watched, horrified, until the raccoon finally froze, and was still.

Dead?

Then there was the sound of wings. Out of nowhere, a

hawk flapped down, holding one leg to its body. It poked the raccoon, and when it got no response, looked around at the rest of the scene. For a while, it stood, and then it looked straight at Lysander, just visible inside the cave. If Lysander had been out in the open, the hawk would have gone straight for him. As it was, Lysander was safe.

"You win, bunny." It said, "But I kill, some day." It screeched, and took off, heading for the morning sun. Had it actually gone?

After an eternity, Lysander took a few cautious steps out to see it all for himself. Somewhere down the riverbank Arlen was probably dying, but from his spot Lysander saw the body of the huge, sick raccoon, dead. The thin white body of Mirada lay a few yards away, and Lysander saw her chest moving, just the tiniest bit. Darshep groaned to the other side, lying on his back, eyes misty.

How had this happened? Lysander took a few cautious steps, feeling an almost forgotten feeling in his chest. His heart seemed to be screaming, in horrible pain. The feeling was so intense Lysander collapsed for a second. His body was fine, but he could barely make himself move. He felt so... so...

Slowly, Lysander realized that it was his fault. Everything that had happened, the bats, the hawk, the raccoon... and this fight. It was his fault. Immediately after the realization came the tears. Then sobbing, racking his body.

"Lysander." A voice said. Lysander looked up, wondering where it had come from.

It whispered again, "Lysander, over here." Lysander looked at the noise to see the huge mass of the raccoon. He yelped, scrambling back. His heart seemed to shred from the effort. It wasn't the raccoon, though. It was coming from behind the raccoon. Lysander went around it, looking in every direction, but saw nothing.

"Lysander."

He looked, took a few hops, and saw. It was Fallon. Lysander went to his side. The bat was paralyzed, wings bent in every direction. When the raccoon had attacked, it must have gone straight over him.

"Well." The bat stared at Lysander with the eye that wasn't facing the ground, "I guess that's it. That was my last try. You beat me."

"I…" Lysander bit his lip, "Sorry."

"Well! Learned something, have we?" The bat grinned a tiny grin, still prone on the ground. Lysander sat down to get nearer to its face.

"I started all this. All of it."

"Yes, though I continued it. The hawk and the raccoon, my fault." Fallon said, closing his eyes, "Which I must apologize for. I was foolish, I thought I could control it."

"They all protected me. I didn't even get hurt." Lysander said, crying again, "Why?"

"Darshep and Arlen will live. Well, they might, at least."

Lysander sobbed, "What about… Mira?"

"Her?" Fallon sighed, "Half-starved and bit clean through? She's probably infected. You can't fight rabies. If she does survive, that'll kill her anyway. She'll have to be thrown in the river so nobody else gets sick. Your girlfriend's gone, friend."

Lysander stopped sobbing, "What?"

"Oh, right." Fallon breathed out slowly, "You didn't know."

Lysander stared, wondering what he meant. Then, like the lightning bolt that had shocked straight through his brain, the

obvious hit him. He gasped, "Oh *no.*"

"I hear she had a thing for you since the moment you showed up. Pity you never knew. Now it's gone. You didn't even know her full name was Mirada, did you?"

"No. No, I can't."

"What? Does the great Lysander have a way to stop even rabies?" Fallon asked, then laughed. Lysander didn't answer, wondering, even hoping. There had to be a way. Fallon coughed, hacking out his next words, "I think I'm going to be gone soon, too. Tell Arlen he's in charge…" He closed his eyes, breathing slowly, "And tell him I said hello to mom."

Fallon took another breath, and lay still. Lysander bowed his head for a moment in silence. The only sounds on the whole mountain were a soft wind, an even softer breath of Darshep's, and Lysander's screaming, screaming emotions. Rage, fear, and hate. Hate for himself. But mostly sadness, grief. Not like those pathetic words could compare, though.

It was all his fault.

Lysander turned, sprinting for his cave, trying not to think. If he did, he would freeze, he wouldn't know what to do. He got inside, and moved down to his cell phone next to the computer. He dialed Drew's number.

"Odd?"

"Listen, I need help. Don't argue, please." Lysander said through his tears, dropping into human voice.

"What? Are you okay?"

"There are three bunnies… and a bat, heavily injured at this location." Lysander said, looking up GPS coordinates on his computer and relaying them, "There is also another bat and a raccoon, but they're dead. One of the hurt bunnies might have rabies. Got all that?"

"What—"

"Get a vet! Pay them anything, just make sure it's the best. And they need to hurry. Fast." Lysander said, and hung up. He took a long, slow breath. The hope was worse now. There wasn't much of a chance, but now there was one. That made it hurt more, if that was possible. The uncertainty.

Then, he turned to his computer, realizing it was done. He could let it go right now. He had to.

Hating himself, Lysander clicked a few buttons, and left the cave. It was out of his hands now. So this was what being helpless felt like, he mused sickly.

CHAPTER 37

"Just following orders, I guess."

–Drew Howell

The vets arrived in a white truck, dust pouring off the back end as they roared up the mountain. They piled out, grabbed some equipment, and ran, following a GPS.

"There's that raccoon!" One yelled, pointing. They scattered, checking the raccoon and then putting it in a plastic bag. Darshep was loaded into a cage with Lysander, who pretended to have fainted. Darshep groaned, hissing as they picked him up, but had no strength to stop them. Lysander saw the terror in his eyes, but didn't know what to say that could counter a lifetime of fearing humans. Mirada was put in her one cage, but was unconscious and didn't make a sound. Her fur was streaked red, angry wounds along her body. With terror, Lysander saw the clear gleam of saliva tracing the wounds. Rabies.

"That doesn't look good." The vet said, every word a knife in Lysander's side, "What happened to it?"

Fallon's body was found, and put in another plastic bag. Lysander wondered what they planned to do with him. That just made him cry again, though, so he stopped. They couldn't find Arlen for a while, and to Lysander's horror started to talk

about leaving without the last bat, get the others to the hospital fast. Finally, he was found, and put in a birdcage. Then it was off to the truck. They were loaded in the back, and the engine started, rumbling and shaking the cages. A vet sat in the back of the truck, holding the cages steady and looking in on them.

"I'm going to die." Darshep said softly, groaning.

"You'll be fine." Lysander said.

"The humans caught us." Darshep said.

"I know. I came along."

"You want to die? Not smart." Darshep said. He groaned, curling up in pain. Lysander saw nothing wrong on the outside of Darshep's body, which worried him even more. Where was Darshep's injury, and how bad was it? Internal bleeding was even serious in humans, but Lysander knew that animals didn't get nearly as good treatment. While a human got an ambulance and an entire team of doctors, animals got truck beds and maybe one doctor. Of course, he couldn't tell Darshep that. Lysander knew he had to lie, and hated himself for it. Just one more black mark on his useless soul. He hadn't cared about his soul for so long, he wasn't even sure if he still had one.

Lysander said, "They aren't going to kill us."

Darshep frowned, "You... arranged this?"

Lysander bit his lip, "Yes."

"This is madness."

"They'll help you. Mirada too."

"How can I trust you?"

"I... I'm here with you, and I know how Mirada feels." Lysander looked down, knowing Darshep wasn't believing him. He added, "You also have no choice."

"I'll believe the last part." Darshep said, before hissing out a breath. He grimaced, closing his eyes, "I told Tysell... that I'd

see her. I have to see her again."

"You will. I promise. Just... wait." Lysander said hesitantly, his words insufficient, the apology in the back of his throat refusing to come out.

Darshep waited. Lysander turned, looking through the slit of his cage at the wire cage that contained Mirada. She was barely breathing, blood slow but still leaking. He looked up at the vet, who stared down at him, surprised by his movement.

"You don't look so hurt anymore." The vet said, "Your pals don't look good, though. Especially this one." She patted the wire cage.

Lysander looked away. He didn't want the human to see him crying.

The truck moved off the mountain, then through the town. Then it stopped. Lysander looked around. What was going on? The vet sitting in the truck by his cage seemed to have the same question. The truck door opened, and several people got out, though Lysander couldn't see too well. There was talking, which evolved into shouting, but it was still incoherent. There was some kind of growing white noise, which they had been driving towards this entire time. Lysander tried to figure out what it was, but couldn't quite do it.

Finally, the vets began to pile back into the truck. The one by Lysander yelled, "Hey! What's happening?"

"The entire section of town is closed, for that big speech by that Odd person!" A person shouted back, "No getting on the highway, either, there's too many cars coming in. It's evolved into a total traffic jam."

"What are we going to do with the bunnies?" The vet asked. She got no answer, instead the door slammed and the truck took a u-turn. It drove a short distance, then stopped.

The engine puttered to a sloppy halt. The vet by Lysander got out along with the others, and they stood in a circle, talking.

Lysander stared. He couldn't think. He couldn't see a way out. He was sure there was one, but his mind was blank. Whenever he tried to think, all that appeared in his mind was memories. Mostly of Mirada, smiling, helping, always happy. Trying to impress.

He had been a fool, not seeing that. He had become the robot again, just like he had been at the pet store. Lysander remembered better now, the shock arousing his memories. His parents, how much he had loved them.

Then they were taken away, taken just like every brother and sister and leaving only him.

Alone, day in, day out homesickness, boredom that evolved into longing that evolved into a painful ache. An ache that had grown worse and worse, until it was too much to bear.

That was when Lysander made the decision he would no longer bear it. He trained himself, grew into a routine that could be followed without a single thought to run it. It had been easy, he had always had quite a steady routine even within his own family. They had joked he could do it in his sleep.

So he did. His entire life became a waking sleep.

That's what he had done the second time, this time. He had almost begun to care, almost became attached to the other bunnies, new friends. But something was wrong. The wilds were a dangerous place, a place where the greatest friend could die just by bad luck. Lysander wasn't sure if he could handle that. Besides that, they all stared at him, like a freak. He hadn't realized it at first, but he was a freak. He understood things that weren't meant for a bunny. He cracked the human language and even began to understand things beyond what he could see. He was special, whether for good or for bad, and he could never, ever belong. Not that way.

So, Lysander did it again. He stopped thinking. He set his mind to a task that his heart believed impossible. He told it to destroy, to defeat the humans. That was impossible, of course.

Lysander had underestimated himself. As he let his heart sleep, feelings buried beneath layers of cruelty and narrow-mindedness, his mind set out for the task, and actually did it. Now, in just about half an hour, it was going to begin. Lysander wasn't sure what it would look like, but he was sure it wasn't going to be good.

Now, his heart had come into the open, shocked out of hiding. It saw what Lysander had done, and ached. All Lysander could see through the tiny slit of his cage was a horribly injured Mirada, one who wouldn't get the help she desperately needed. She had followed her heart, and his brain had killed it.

Lysander sobbed, begging himself, his heart asking, pleading for a solution. It tittered, seemed to skip a beat. The white noise, which Lysander recognized now as a moving crowd, seemed to grow deafening. In frustration, Lysander smacked his head against the wall of the cage.

Lightning blasted across his mind, shot from the black scar he had just smashed into the wall. His heart seemed to stop, giving Lysander an odd, clenched feeling in his chest. Then it started again, and Lysander realized he had the answer. It sounded stupid, almost impossible.

But for Lysander, impossible wasn't really a word.

CHAPTER 38

"Why is it that we always say, 'Wait! I changed my mind!' the exact second it becomes too late?"

–Lysander

The cage lock was just a little hook through a loop, taking only thirty seconds for Lysander to unfasten. It was good that most animals were stupid enough that that worked, otherwise Lysander might have been stopped before he even started. He hopped on top of his cage, jumping on the bed of the truck and scrambling down as fast as he could without falling. Then, vets noticing and jumping after him to catch him, he ran. Ran as fast and as hard as he could.

It got hard fast.

Lysander knew where he was headed. The auditorium on the second floor of the BunnyWorks skyscraper. That's where the press conference would be, the one Drew had been expecting him to be at. For once, Drew was going to get what he wanted. Or at least, what he had asked for. Lysander began to have difficulties before he even was within three blocks.

It was the people. The white noise turned out to be a crowd so massive that it covered entire blocks. Multiple languages babbled excitedly to each other. Police were setting up barriers frantically, using road construction signs and tape.

People in polo shirts sporting the BunnyWorks logo were setting up large sound sets and televisions everywhere, trying to make it so everyone that wasn't going to get inside could watch. Above it all loomed the black and grey building, plastered with his signs, his advertisements he had ordered but never seen for himself.

The smell of noonday sun on tarmac mixed with sweat hung low on the ground, heat searing the bottoms of Lysander's paws. The people talked, always talking.

Lysander was flattered. Was he really this popular?

That thought was crushed as a foot slammed down next to Lysander, nearly crushing him as well. Lysander gasped, looking up into the face of a thoroughly confused man.

"Rabbit?" He said.

Lysander bolted. He kept running, jumping over or under feet, hurrying as fast as he could. There was no telling how much time this would take. Every second it took was a second less that Mirada could get to the hospital. Lysander told himself that over and over. She would get to the hospital. He would make sure she made it that far. No, he would make sure she made it all the way.

His heart jumping up his throat, Lysander turned a corner and saw the massive monolith. Its glass shone on the bright morning sun, rising towards the center of the sky. It was probably near time for the press conference.

Lysander arrived at the building and shot through the security lines. People yelled, pointed at the intruder. Some leaned down to grab him, but it was impossible. Lysander was too small, too low to the ground and too unexpected. Almost every security table didn't touch the ground, and there was always a gap between a guard's legs. Lysander made it to the lobby and kept going. He smiled as he ran, loving the feel of the carpet. Whatever interior designers Drew had hired did a good job, at least by his standards. The sleek chrome and glass tables caught his fancy. Very modern.

Odd knew the floor layout, and took several rights, going straight through all the people in the halls. His heart screamed for mercy, pounding, pounding, but he didn't listen. He could make it. Just a little farther. Lysander hit the stairs, and began to haul his way up them, not slowing down at all. He felt his heart tripping, but refused to stop. There wasn't time. He had to make it, and the glimpses of clocks from the corners of his eyes said there wasn't any time to spare.

Lysander saw the door he wanted ahead, held open by the security guard for none other than Drew Howell. Drew smiled nervously, dressed in a suit far too expensive to logically be worn more than once, if ever. Lysander went straight through the gap between them. Behind, the security guard shouted, "Vermin!"

Drew froze, staring after Lysander. As Lysander kept moving, he could swear he heard Drew say, "Glossy?"

Lysander took note of the stage, and the new equipment backstage, never before used. He scrambled under a bundle of bags, and peeked out, waiting.

Drew made a move to follow Lysander, but was stopped by a man wearing a headset. The man pointed towards the stage urgently.

Music began to play through the overhead speakers, and Drew strolled onto the stage. The audience erupted into cheers and applause. Drew waited for a reasonable amount of silence, and began, "Thank you for all coming to this big, big day."

The audience cheered again.

"As you all know, I have invited Odd to come out today, in person, to show himself for the very first time. I'm sure he won't disappoint. Now, he isn't here yet, but we are a little behind schedule. We didn't expect the huge crowd you see in the streets, and are still setting up some TV monitors and speakers for them all. But we will start when Odd arrives. He is sure to be here, any minute, and I will introduce him to you all. Excuse me a moment." Drew practically jogged off the stage. He left an almost visible trail of worry and sweat in his wake.

He ran for the cluster of assistants and experts, "Has anyone seen him?" Drew used a cuff to wipe his brow, and Lysander winced as he watched. So much for that suit.

"No sir." an assistant answered, "One man down at security claims he is Odd, but he sounds nothing like him and is roughly ninety years old. We think he might be senile, sir."

"Well, I guess we just wait. I hope…" Drew trailed off. He wiped his brow again.

Lysander, under the bags, took a deep, long breath. Then he let it out. He repeated this several times, trying to calm himself. His heart didn't seem to have slowed down at all. But none of that mattered, because Lysander had come too far to make it here. He began to slowly move forward, moving to the gap in the curtains at the center of the stage.

Lysander went out, blinking in the blinding spotlights, and began to hop forward. He hopped for the podium in the center of the stage. Then, realizing he could never hop on top, went around it to the front of the stage. Lysander took a position in front of the floor mikes, breathing in yet another breath. The breath caused a low rush over the sound system, like an unexpected wind.

The audience was laughing.

Lysander opened his eyes. What was going on? Then he realized what it had to be. They thought it was some kind of joke. This was *BunnyWorks*, after all. They saw him as a mascot, perhaps. Entertainment until Odd arrived. They had no idea. No one had any idea. Drew and some guards watched, but they made no move to stop him. They didn't know what to think. Neither did Lysander. He was sick of using his brain, now he was just going to go with whatever else there was. Maybe that could reverse it.

As horrible as everything was, Odd had to fight not to grin. This was going to get interesting.

"Hello." Odd said.

Silence.

"My name is Lysander. But I have a nickname." Lysander said, "A rather... *Odd* nickname."

The audience was frozen. There were a few gasps, whispers. Even a giggle. But mostly silence. Some were slack jawed, all were paying attention. Quite a reaction, even from what Lysander had expected.

"Look, I don't have much time. I have... an emergency, and I have to get to it fast. Besides that, for certain other reasons... our time is going to be cut short. You probably have questions. Most of them are probably about my appearance. What you see is what I am. No tricks, no ventriloquism. I'm a bunny, okay? Plain and simple. Yes, I talk. I learned to talk after I was hit by a power line. I think that messed with my brain a little. It made me smarter. You should try it." Lysander grinned, "That was a joke. Sorry, not too good at humor."

There was a laugh, somewhere out in the crowd. Even the whispering had stopped. Lysander looked behind, at the massive television bank behind him. That was probably what

was doing it. His face was blown up a thousand times its size, allowing the audience to see him pronounce every single word, no ventriloquism. Maybe they thought he was animation. A hologram, or something.

"Look, I have to tell you something, before I go. You deserve to know." Lysander bowed his head, "You've all been wanting to know why I do what I do. Why I give away everything I make for free, and let Mr. Howell take all the credit. Well, the reality is that it was all a lie. I wasn't what I said I was. Sure, I wanted to stay out of the limelight, but the reason for that is so that you wouldn't be able to find me. I wanted to disappear."

Lysander took a deep breath, noticing that his heart was now at a somewhat slow, steady pace. He felt oddly calm. The speakers crackled with static, but quieted again. This was it, for good or bad. He began the final stretch, "I wanted to have a global presence in every computer around the world connected to the internet. This included phones, GPS's, even cars and fridges, if they were advanced enough. I planted in every one of my computers a set of code. You all know how my computers can change code to fit them? Run any program? Well, they can also change a program so that it runs on any other computer. You didn't know that, because I made it so you wouldn't know. I didn't want you to see it coming."

The lights flickered, buzzing oddly. The audience murmured, and Lysander turned to look behind him. Drew stood at the edge of the stage, face emotionless but plainly shocked. Above him, the bank of televisions had lost a monitor, a black square where Lysander's fur had used to be.

Lysander turned to the microphone, "I infected every computer I could with a virus. It's indestructible by your standards, impossible to stop. It becomes your computer, replacing every piece of programming in it with my own programming. Then it begins to destroy itself."

The lights pulsed brightly, one popping and sending down a shower of sparks. The audience gasped. Lysander continued, "I didn't mean to come here today, but I had too. I don't have time to explain why. I just had to warn you. It's been activated, and it's working right now. All I can say is… well… I'm sorry." Lysander hung his head, but the tears wouldn't come. He was out of tears, even, "This is what I think you all call deathbed repentance. But for what it's worth… I am truly sorry. I see that now.

"You'll hate me, I know. I can take that, I've been either hated or ignored my whole life. I lost everything because I was such an idiot I didn't see the thing right in front of me. So, sorry. I am so, so… sorry. And… and… goodbye."

Lysander turned, running towards the back of the stage. His heart was pumping fast again, audible if it weren't for the sounds of crowd babble, screams as the lights flashed angrily and bulbs blew. It was working. Not that it had any chance of failing, of course. Lysander cursed his brilliance.

Then he came to the feet of Drew Howell, stopping and looking up. For a long time, they just looked at each other. Eventually, Glossy said, "And especially to you, friend. I owe you a special apology."

Drew dropped to his knees, stretching out a hand to Lysander. Then he pulled it back, "Glossy?"

The lights buzzed, several more popping and letting out a cascade of sparks. The speakers overloaded, and blasted a high pitched squeal. People screamed, covering their ears and faces.

Above it all, Lysander yelled, "I think we better get go-

ing!"

Drew Howell nodded, grabbing Lysander. Lysander squeaked in shock, terror flooding through him at the sudden manhandling. He barely controlled the instinct not to bite Drew. Drew shifted Lysander, folding him in his arms just like he used to at the pet shop so long ago, and ran from the building. He ran for his life. For Drew, it was simply following orders. He knew that voice, and now that he saw the face... he felt fine. They were just old friends, after all.

CHAPTER 39

"Sometimes, we get used to power. We forget that our followers have their own minds, and treat them like robots. And who expects a robot to fight its master?"

–Lysander

"Out of the way! Out!" Drew shouted, shoving people aside with one arm as he raced down the hall. His other arm held Lysander.

"We need to get on ground level!" Lysander yelled.

"I always knew you were weird, Glossy!" Drew said, yelling above the din. The lights blacked out, throwing the hall into darkness. It became a jumble of yelling, shouting bodies. The P.A. system was dinging off every note imaginable, but in no order and at max volume.

"I was expecting you to panic." Lysander shouted.

"I thought you were dead... but I know that voice." Drew said, "I can't deny it's you. No one else could cause all this either, all these lights and everything..."

"Even though I'm a bunny? Stairs! You missed the stairs!"

"Sorry." Drew turned, doubling back and getting on the stairs, he shouted several times, and barged down them shoving people out of the way. Everyone seemed to be trying to get out at once. Drew said, "I don't know. I'm trying not to think about it. If I did, I might lose my mind!"

Lysander chuckled, "I do that too. Not thinking, I mean."

Drew got on the main floor, sprinting across the carpet and even clearing a couch in the lobby as he ran for the doors, "Where are we going?"

"I called you this morning, about some bunnies? One is named Mirada. She's sick, but we can't get her out of here with the highway jammed. She needs a vet."

Drew sucked in a breath, gasping out his words as he sprinted, "Oh… a bunny, I didn't think… that important… but I guess… it is."

The crowd outside was in uproar. The police had retreated, merely trying not to get run over in the huge stampede. The lights all over Helaman Valley were going crazy. Smoke poured out of two or three windows, car alarms shrilling over and over. One car, shiny and new, turned on by itself and revved forward, slamming the car parked in front of it and totaling them both.

"This is bad." Drew said. Lysander shot him a look, but refrained from insulting Drew's obvious comment.

"It's going to get worse. Left!" Lysander said. Drew turned, forcing his way through the panicking crowd. Lysander almost expected them to recognize him and Drew, stop them and demand they fix it. But it was all too confused. No one was concerned about anything but getting away. Cell phone ringtones formed a cloud of tinny musical notes, going off without any calls, vibrating for no reason, shocking owners with static electricity through their pockets. Lysander prayed that Drew could find a way through it all. He was going well, arm cushioning Lysander from the mass of people, but it was still a long way to the vet truck.

"So this is why… *BunnyWorks*, huh?"

"I'm conceited, I guess." Lysander grinned, "Would you

like it to be called *Drew's Computers?*"

"I'll take a pass on that." Drew said, "Thanks, by the way."

Lysander blinked, "For what?"

"You aren't yelling at me for once."

Lysander grinned weakly, "Not much of a choice. You might get mad and drop me."

"Not a chance." Drew grinned, "You're healthy, even free range. Probably worth 30 bucks!"

"That'd be nice." Lysander said. He tried to think of something else to say. He had to keep Drew talking, his mind occupied. If he didn't, Drew might realize what was going on, actually try to think it through. Then would come either shock or panic or both.

So Lysander kept talking, kept light and cheerful, as Drew shoved, fought, drove forward through the crowd. It went on for a long time. Then, it began to clear. Drew began to run again, then sprint. Lysander bounced up and down in his arms, gritting his teeth.

"There. That truck."

Drew ran up, unceremoniously dumping Lysander in the back. He leaned over the side, checking to make sure the cages were still all there, still had the occupants inside.

"Hey!" A vet ran up, "Get out of there! Those are pa-tients!" He looked into the truck, "Hey, the white one's back." Then he looked up at Drew, "You're… that famous guy."

"Yeah." Drew said, "Glossy, what next? Where do we go?"

"We need to get out of here." Lysander said. The vet visibly paled, but Lysander ignored him, "We need to get Mirada, her—" He pointed, "To the vet! Now!"

"That bunny isn't… it can't be…" The vet looked over at Drew in confusion, "T-talking?"

"Of course it—" Drew paled, obviously truly realizing for the first time what was going on. He looked down at Lysander again, "Glossy?"

Drew fainted. The vet ducked down to him, trying to catch him as he fell but instead just going down with him. Lysander's throat twisted as he looked back at the still-unconscious Mirada. She was unconscious, of course. Lysander kept telling himself that, hoping it was still true.

But true for how long?

Lysander jumped onto the lip of the truck. Drew was lying across the road, screaming people rushing past on both sides, cars out of commission. Stores were lighting on fire all over from electric shorts, loud sirens and static blasting at max over the speakers. The electricity was still flowing in, fueling the destruction. The running people were even causing damage. And as it all happened, Lysander just stood, staring.

This wasn't working.

Lysander jumped, as hard as he could. He arced through the air, gasping as the ground rose to meet him. He landed right on Drew's face, smashing and bouncing off of it. For a few seconds, he lay immobile on the ground. It hurt to move, even to stay still.

A bunny. So high and mighty, yet so fragile.

After a few seconds, he battled up, up through the lightning-laced pain, and moved to his feet. Another vet stared at him, waiting for him to do something, in total shock.

"A little room, please?" Lysander asked politely. Screaming in absolute horror, the vet ran. Lysander scooted over a few inches, gasping from the effort, until his nose was right up to Drew's ear.

"Drew…" Lysander wheezed, "I… I know this is hard,

and overwhelming, and crazy… but… you owe me. See, I made this business and I…" Lysander stopped, "No, scratch all that.

"I'm that bunny, Drew, that little bunny in the pet store. I've changed, I've grown and made mistakes… I made one right now. I thought if I finished the press conference fast enough all the people would leave and I could get out of here. But I was too late! And now, I just want you to be that person again. I want you to pick me up, save me… save my friends. Care for us like you used to. Drew, do you remember? You remember?

Drew groaned. Lysander added, "For me, Glossy."

Drew opened his eyes.

Moments later, Drew was on his feet again. Lysander in one arm, he shoved through the crowd to the vet truck. The windows had been smashed by the frantic crowd, but there were fewer now, enough that it was possible to breathe again. They were losing time. As Drew hoisted the wire cage, yelling at the vets who hadn't run off to come and help, Lysander could only stare at the thin, dirty body… and hope.

"My jet! Private jet!" Drew yelled to the vets, "We'll never be able to drive out!"

The vets nodded, and ran. Lysander yelled to Drew, "Give me your phone!

Drew handed off the wire cage, and pulled out his phone. Lysander grabbed it, and once again summoned all of his wits. He tapped, clicked, typed, and hoped. Hoped that it would be enough.

Hope.

Before, he had thought there would be no hope. But for Odd, all he really needed, all he had ever needed, was a keyboard, a screen, an internet connection.

And the newest *BunnyWorks* phone had all those things.

As they ran, the world seemed to dim. Screams faded, music stopped playing. At first it seemed to be the fact that they were getting farther away from town. But then, the streetlights stopped flickering, the telephone lines stopped sparking from overload. The world grew quiet, screams fading into yells, which slowly lapsed into sobs. Sobs of scared people, worried, hoping it was over but not quite sure. Drew crested the steps to his plane as Lysander tapped in the last command.

Wireless internet was truly the most wonderful thing on Earth.

Drew started the plane, Lysander taking a place next to him. After Drew shut the door so the vets in the back couldn't hear, Lysander said, "I think that should do it. The virus should turn off now, delete itself."

"See? I knew you could do it, Glossy! And we'll make sure your girlfriend is safe and sound too." Drew said, "Just stop talking. It's freaky enough flying a plane, you keep talking and I'll probably go insane. I'm just glad my father taught me how to… he was a crop duster, you know… never mind." Drew shook his head, muttering about bunnies, knuckles white on the controls.

Odd smiled, a tiny, weak, tired smile. Then he picked the phone up in his teeth, hopping down to the seat. He turned on the phone again and got to work. He had a bit of hacking to do. Nuclear bombs were controlled by computer, meaning every single one had been either activated or fired. Lysander thought it would probably be a good idea to sink them in the ocean before they blew up millions of people. Lysander wondered if he should tell Drew.

No, he had enough to worry about.

CHAPTER 40

"One day, that Odd character is going to realize he can't have everything. Then, maybe, we can all get a break."

–Cory Yalk

Winter was drawing its cloak over everything once again. A lot had happened over the past months, mostly repairs across the world, fixing everything that was broken. In other words, basically everything except the roads, but sometimes even those. Formal apologies were made. Drew was arrested and questioned on suspicion of terrorism. But one day he was released suddenly, the only clue to why being the arrival of Cory Yalk at FBI headquarters. Cory had talked to a few people, and suddenly Drew was free to go.

Before he left, Cory came up to him. They stood in the hallway, computers lying in pieces all around as technicians poked around inside to see the damage. Construction noises blazed through the walls, but people kept their voices low. Subdued, even.

"How?" Was all Drew could make himself say.

"Haven't you wondered about me, friend?" Cory grinned, donning a pair of sunglasses, "I tell you I'm just a simple reporter. I sneak around, know things I shouldn't. I even know criminal psychology. But still, just a reporter. Or so I said.

We're always watching, Drew.

"Oh, and a tip. If you ever meet Odd, ever find out anything about him? Better tell us before we find out you didn't."

Drew had almost laughed at that. No one was ever going to find Odd. They had already found him, but didn't know it. They said the press conference had been some kind of animation, a hologram invented by whoever Odd was. They all thought he was still out there, somewhere. But when they asked Drew, all he could tell them was the truth. Odd valued his privacy, he would say. He didn't know where or who Odd was, and had no way of finding out. Odd wouldn't even answer his cell phone, he said.

There was a reason for that, of course. Drew had Lysander's cell phone, along with every single computer and device that Lysander's cave had held. Lysander had given Drew instructions, even came along to go down the tunnel and pull it all out. Drew was the only one there, of course, but then of course he was the only one that believed. Besides that, he had taken almost a week alone before even getting used to the thought. Talking to bunnies was something that took getting used to.

A lot had happened at the bunny caves, as well. Darshep, after a speedy recovery, came with Lysander on his trip to pick up all his computer stuff. Tysell had been waiting at the mouth of the tunnels, ducking in fright when she saw Drew. When Darshep came out of a pet carrier, though, she ran right across to him, heedless of danger. Lysander only heard Darshep say, "I promised, remember?" After nuzzling noses quickly, and with several nervous glances at Drew, they went back into the caves. Drew just stared, no idea what was going on.

Arlen had recovered eventually, and flew back home to Darkdoor. From what Lysander had last heard, Arlen had de-

livered the news of Fallon's death before taking his place. He led the bats, an easy job right now since it was simply hibernation time. Come summer, his job would certainly become harder. The last time Lysander had seen him was on the ride away from emptying his cave. Arlen sat by the side of the road, roosting in a tree, head bowed. Beneath him lay a stone slab, a simple silhouette of a bat carved into it. Fallon's grave, placed at the spot where the car had taken both of Arlen's parents.

Arlen had been what originally gave Lysander the idea. His very last idea. Arlen had suffered more than anyone else, Lysander knew. He had done it not out of revenge or his own mistakes, but out of pure kindness, even to people who just hurt him in return. Lysander was one of those. Lysander hoped that maybe some of the hurt could be repaired, if only a tiny fraction, by his plan. He had made so many plans to hurt people, maybe it was time to do one to help.

There was a lot of pain, Lysander knew. He even felt sorry for the raccoon, buried in a shallow grave with no marking at all, a few feet from the entrance of Lysander's cave, the exact place he had died. Darshep, Tysell, and all the bunnies had watched. There was even a hawk in a nearby tree, head bowed but still watching. Lysander had been glad Drew was there, digging the grave.

Of course, if someone drove up there now, there wouldn't be anything. No caves, no bunnies. There were still the waterfalls, of course. Waterlog looked just as beautiful in winter as anytime. But it was abandoned. Even Darkdoor was vacant, the place where the bats had roosted now completely empty, in a time when they should have been hibernating. The bats and bunnies had moved on, led by Darshep and Arlen, following instructions from Lysander. He only hoped they had made it.

"*Did* they make it?" He asked. He was sitting in passenger seat of a sports car, driven by Drew. Drew twitched a little, as he always did when Lysander talked to him. Lysander shifted, his paws squeaking against the Italian leather. Drew finally sighed, getting ready to talk and probably telling himself that he wasn't crazy, that the bunny really was talking and it wasn't all in his head.

"They all made it. They're all there, the bats hibernating, the bunnies settling in." Drew said, and grinned, "You'll be just fine, I think."

"Thank you so much."

"No, thank you." Drew grinned, "It's been a pleasure doing business with you, Glossy."

Lysander smiled, turning away. The car hummed softly, crunching over a gravel road. Trees passed on either side, "I hope people aren't talking too much about it."

"Not too much. They just think I'm an eccentric rich guy with a pet bunny and way too much money to spend." Drew said.

Lysander nodded, letting a few moments pass in silence. Then he nodded to himself, and looked over at Drew, "There's something I need to talk to you about."

"What?"

Lysander explained, "In all my electronics you took from my cave, there's a zip drive, white, plugged into the laptop."

"What about it?"

"It's the business plan for *BunnyWorks*, covering the next ten years." Lysander said.

"Oh, Glossy, I don't think I can—"

"No, you misunderstand." Lysander interrupted him, "It *was* for the next six months. But I don't expect you to work that

hard. You need a break. You're rich now, right? That means you should barely work at all. Or so I hear."

Drew laughed, "Okay, I guess I can handle that. Maybe... no, never mind."

"What?"

"I was thinking of, well, opening a pet store." Drew smiled, "That's in bad taste, though. Saying that in front of you. Or even thinking it knowing what I know now."

"No... well, most animals aren't like me. I'm... well, you know." Lysander shrugged, looking down, "To be honest, living in a cage isn't fun. It is safe, though, and you'll live a lot longer. There are pros and cons, I guess. I've been in both, and made the same mistakes both times, so it doesn't really matter how an animal lives, it's just that you have to figure out how to be happy with whatever circumstances. You have to find something that makes you happy. So... if you want a pet shop, if that makes you happy, go for it." Lysander smiled, "But if you do, make sure to build about fifty of them. You certainly have the budget for it."

"I only want one. Just... for myself." Drew said, "Besides that, I think we've arrived."

CHAPTER
41

"Every time you say hello, realize that means you're going to have to say goodbye someday. Not that that's a bad thing, after all, you can always say hello again."

–Arlen

Drew parked the car, getting out and holding the door open for Lysander. After Lysander was out, he picked up a box from the back seat, gently cradling it under one arm. The car was parked in a simple gravel lot. The forest trees crowded all around, blocking the horizon. Ahead of them was a large gate house, heavy fences extending either side away from it. A security guard at the gate checked a pass of Drew's, and the gates opened with a low, electronic hum. Lysander went through first, Drew following. The guards stared behind them, at Drew a little but mostly at the weird little bunny that seemed to be leading him.

Lysander smiled. He stood in front of a large valley. Little blobs of trees sprung up here and there, little batches of dark among the glimmering snow. The snow arced on for hills and hills, dotted by little black freckles. Each freckle was an entrance to an elaborate cave system, dug by special human machines. The entire area had been landscaped as well, and come summer was going to sprout a horde of grass, flowers, and edible plants.

A river, rimmed with ice just as it would be rimmed with

moss come summer, languidly stretched, going back and forth across the valley. Over at the fence line in the distance, a large dam had been erected. The water was controlled, always slow enough that it could never pose any danger. The fence by the dam rimmed the valley on three sides. The fourth had a stark cliff face, fresh drill marks scarring the rock. A number of large caves had been bored into the mountain, and inside one of them Lysander knew a certain group of bats were hibernating for the winter.

"Okay, here you go, then." Drew said, leaning down. He set the box on the grounds, ripping off the two pieces of tape that held the side on. Then he opened the box, and stood back.

"Mirada?" Lysander said, looking in the box, "It's me, Lysander. We're here."

Out of the box came a white nose, followed by the head of Mirada. She took a cautious glance around, then caught sight of Drew. Yelping, she ducked back inside.

"No, it's okay." Lysander said, "He's that human I told you about, the one that's helping us. That's why I had you get in the box, Mirada, so that he wouldn't scare you, and the car ride wouldn't be so bad. It's okay, though. Now you can come out."

Slowly, Mirada crept out, keeping a close eye on Drew the whole time. Her face was scared, eyes red and sickly. Her body was covered with patches of scars, places hair would never grow, scabs that might not ever heal. She was still thin, but not nearly as thin as before. What fur she did have was every bit as white as Lysander's, if not as shiny.

All his fault.

"You look great." Lysander told her. He had made sure she never saw a mirror at the vets' office. Eventually, she would see

her reflection in a pool or puddle, but not for a while. Lysander planned to make sure of that. For now, she needed to think she was beautiful, and she was.

She smiled at his comment, looking around. Her smile turned into a look of wonder, "What—"

"Drew set it up. Caves for the bats, bunny holes everywhere. When it's summer, there is going to be so much food that we'll never have to worry. Drew even made sure there was plenty of food in the caves, and he'll have some people check up on us every two weeks, just too make sure. And you know what else?"

"What?" Mirada asked breathlessly.

"No predators." Lysander said, "The fence keeps them out, and they've got some people with guns to keep them out. They can even tranquilize birds… that means, they can catch them and move them so far away they'll never come back. If anything does get in, well, there are so many caves you won't have to run three feet before you're safe."

"Oh…" Mirada said. She kept looking around, her breath misting on the freezing air, "It's cold."

"It'll be warmer in the caves." Lysander suggested. Mirada nodded, and they slowly moved across the field, towards a hole only ten feet away. Lysander looked back, nodding. Drew picked up the box, waved, and left. The gates clanged shut.

Lysander could only wonder if they'd ever see each other again.

The caves were large, dug by humans instead of rabbits. But they were a little warmer. There were even heaters somewhere, Drew said. Mirada looked around, as if finally realizing where they were, "No predators."

"Nothing." Lysander said.

Mirada smiled, "Lysander, I always hoped, always..."

"Mirada, I want to say something." Lysander interrupted her, "I wanted to tell you before, but I was working on this, and you were at the vet for so long, and... well... Mirada?"

"Yes?" She asked, turning to him. She wasn't smiling, but her face was impassive. Maybe hopeful?

"I never noticed you before, never saw how you acted, how you did everything for me. I'm so sorry, and I'm in your debt. I just, well, I wanted to say that if you want, maybe... maybe we can start over? As friends?" Lysander grimaced, "No, that's not what I meant, I meant... um..." He turned toward a few small bunnies peeking around a corner,

"Can I get a little privacy here?"

The bunnies giggled and ran off.

Lysander took a breath and continued, wondering why his heart was beating so fast and he couldn't seem to talk, "I meant to say, I want, well... I kind of like you, Mirada."

"Kind of like?" Mirada cocked her head.

"I like you."

Mirada nodded, "Okay."

Lysander smiled weakly, heart hammering in his chest, "I really like you."

Mirada's eyes lit up, "Oh!" She grinned, "I guess I kind of like you too."

She smiled wide, her grin crooked with a chipped tooth. Lysander smiled right back, moving closer. Together, they sat, letting the silence fill the cave as snow began to drift through the entrance, their breath creating a thin fog over their heads. Lysander and Mirada huddled closer, sharing their warmth against the cold chill.

As for Lysander, he didn't have a single thought in his

head. It was a total, complete blank, even his headache absent. But he did feel something else, something he had been neglecting for far too long. He was happy. For once, finally and truly happy.

ACKNOWLEDGEMENTS

This book is built on a foundation of help and support from many, many people. I'd like to personally thank a few who helped quite a bit.

My parents, Corinne and Darrel Olsen, who read and reviewed my work from the start and have always offered tons of support.

Shirley Bahlmann, a fantastic author who was always ready with a helping hand and tons of useful information.

Also Elisabeth Frischknecht, my sisters and brothers, and all my friends including Isaiah, Keaton, Gideon and Austin. (All of whom have supported my evil bunny fantasies, and with me, have grown to become Leporiphobiacs.

Additionaly, thanks to our bunnies, cats, turtles, my guinea pig Mandy (now in heaven), and our sugar glider Professor Muffins. I don't know exactly what they did, but this wouldn't feel complete without them, you know?

And thank you, for reading.

NEED MORE?

 LIKE STEVEN OLSEN
ON FACEBOOK

 SUPERSMASHINTERWEB.
COM

 STEVEN OLSEN
ON GOODREADS

KEEP YOUR EYE OUT
FOR NEW RELEASES! I
HOPE YOU ENJOYED THE
BOOK, AND FEEL FREE
TO TELL A FRIEND!

ABOUT THE AUTHOR

Steven Olsen is an up-and-coming author writing science fiction, fantasy, and often a surprising mixture of the two. His books are full of adventure and more than one surprise.

He lives in Southern Utah with his family, is very messy, and honestly doesn't have as much time as television and video games require. But he tries. He also enjoys drawing comics, referring to himself in the third person, the second person, and the omnipresent quasi-narration. Also, he even runs his own comic, which you can see at www.supersmashinterweb.com.

BUNNY MUFFIN BOOKS

www.ingramcontent.com/pod-product-compliance
Lightning Source LLC
Chambersburg PA
CBHW070449120726
47910CB00003B/982

* 9 7 8 0 9 9 0 6 1 1 9 1 2 *